THE SNAKE

MISTAKE

MYSTERY

OTHER GREAT MISTAKE MYSTERIES

The Best Mistake Mystery
The Artsy Mistake Mystery

THE SNAKE

MISTAKE

MYSTERY

THE GREAT MISTAKE
MYSTERIES

sylvia mcnicoll

DUNDURN
TORONTO

Cover image: © Tania Howells
Printer: Webcom

Library and Archives Canada Cataloguing in Publication

McNicoll, Sylvia, 1954-, author
    The snake mistake mystery / Sylvia McNicoll.

(The great mistake mysteries)
Issued in print and electronic formats.
ISBN 978-1-4597-3973-4 (softcover).--ISBN 978-1-4597-3974-1 (PDF).--
ISBN 978-1-4597-3975-8 (EPUB)

I. Title. II. Series: McNicoll, Sylvia, 1954- . Great mistake mysteries.

PS8575.N52S69 2018   jC813'.54   C2017-903395-6
                                               C2017-903396-4

1   2   3   4   5   22   21   20   19   18

 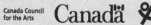

We acknowledge the support of the **Canada Council for the Arts**, which last year invested $153 million to bring the arts to Canadians throughout the country, and the **Ontario Arts Council** for our publishing program. We also acknowledge the financial support of the **Government of Ontario**, through the **Ontario Book Publishing Tax Credit** and the **Ontario Media Development Corporation**, and the **Government of Canada**.

Nous remercions le **Conseil des arts du Canada** de son soutien. L'an dernier, le Conseil a investi 153 millions de dollars pour mettre de l'art dans la vie des Canadiennes et des Canadiens de tout le pays.

Care has been taken to trace the ownership of copyright material used in this book. The author and the publisher welcome any information enabling them to rectify any references or credits in subsequent editions.

— *J. Kirk Howard, President*

VISIT US AT

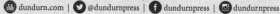

 dundurn.com | @dundurnpress | dundurnpress | dundurnpress

Dundurn
3 Church Street, Suite 500
Toronto, Ontario, Canada
M5E 1M2

For Gisela Tobien Sherman, whose fear of snakes inspired her to write Snake in My Toilet

While the settings and some of the mistakes may be real, the kids, dogs, crossing guards, neighbours, and especially the animal control officer are all made up. If you recognize yourself or anyone else, you've clearly made a mistake. Good for you!

day one

THE GREAT MISTAKE

MYSTERIES

The air feels too warm and heavy for October. The dogs don't even want to walk this morning. It's like they know something.

"What's wrong with them, Stephen?" my friend Renée Kobai asks as she drags Ping out the door. He's the small Jack Russell the Bennetts adopted from the pound, and usually, he sproings out of the house.

"Who cares. They're coming, anyway."

The Bennetts pay Noble Dog Walking, my dad's service, to exercise the dogs for two hours most weekdays. Renée and I work for Dad; we even wear uniforms with the Noble paw print logo. Usually, we take the dogs out for an hour before school and another one after, but today is Saturday. First of a three-day weekend. PA day Monday, yay! Four bonus walks this weekend, morning and afternoon Saturday and Sunday, which means bonus money.

I pull Pong, the Bennetts' long-legged rescue greyhound, out the door. He usually lopes, more often leading us all. But today Pong picks his way through the dry, brown grass, almost tippy-toe.

Ping, the bouncy Jack Russell, digs in with all his strength, mini donkey–style, the whites of his black eyes showing in slivers.

"Move it, Ping. I mean it!" Renée's short, like Ping, and his match in stubbornness.

"Come on, boy," I call softly, feeling a little sorry for him now. "You can't win against Renée."

Finally, his paws stutter forward and he scampers to catch up to Pong. We all head for Brant Hills Park.

The sky looks bruised on one side but sunny over the park. For a while, everything seems perfectly quiet; not even a leaf twitches. Except for Mr. Kowalski jogging beside the fence, all hunched over as usual. Kids call him the hundred-year-old jogger. Not me, though; Renée yelled at me when I did. Mr. K coached Renée's brother, Attila, on his art portfolio and application to Mohawk College. His own paintings are amazing. We have one hanging in our guest room.

We walk along the path up toward the community centre. Maybe we can turn the dogs loose in the tennis court and let them chase a ball.

But then suddenly, the wind blows. Mr. K's black cap flies off, spins in the air, lands, and cartwheels along the ground. It's a Frisbee-sized hat, and the words across it spin — *Pay the Artist, Pay the Artist, Pay the Artist* — into a white blur. Ping makes a break to chase it. I don't know if Renée lets the leash drop on purpose or not. But I drop Pong's, too, and he flies toward the cap as well.

We run after them.

Ping snatches up the cap just as Pong catches up to him. Pong opens his long snout and latches on, too. As his teeth sink into it, there's one frozen moment when I expect it to turn into a big snarl-fest. For sure, when I first started walking them, they would have scrapped over the cap. But today a strange thing happens. Together they carry it back our way. Mr. Kowalski jogs toward us.

"Storm's coming in," he says as the bruises close over the sky and the bright part shrinks. The wind bends the smaller trees backward till they look like their trunks will snap. Any rusty, leftover leaves get shaken to the ground and tossed around.

The dogs don't seem to care about the weather anymore. The cap in their mouths becomes their purpose in life, just like art is to Mr. K. The cap comes within grabbing distance now. "Give it!" I command. Pong lets go. My fingers reach and almost touch the brim when Ping yanks it away. He bows to me, inviting me to play.

"Ping!" I snap my fingers. He freezes for an instant till I reach again, then he dodges.

"No, Ping. Give it."

Ping shakes the cap like it's a rodent he wants to kill.

I reach into my pocket for one of Dad's home-made liver bites.

Ping spits out the cap and sits at attention. Pong joins him, one ear up.

Dad's treats are magic. Dogs will do anything for them. I give each dog a little brown square and grab the leashes.

Meanwhile, Renée snatches up the cap, her nose scrunching in disgust. "Ew. Dog drool." She hands the cap back to Mr. Kowalski.

"Thanks. It's an important hat. Have to remind people, all the time." Mr. K smiles at the wet cap, shakes it off, and jams it back on his head. He taps his brim in a salute. "Better head for cover." Then he chugs off like a very slow train.

Renée and I look up at the sky. It hasn't even been half an hour yet, but the dark side rumbles and throws a yellow pitchfork of lightning at the last tiny patch of brightness.

A few giant raindrops plop onto my hands. "Let's get out of this," I call to Renée as I begin to run.

"Too late!" Renée shouts as the drops patter more quickly.

"Hurry." I keep motoring. The patter turns into a steady drum roll.

Although we run hard back through the park, we can't escape the downpour and quickly go from moist to soggy to soaked. The dogs turn straight into swamp monsters.

Another rumble from the sky ends with such a loud crack that Renée drops the leash to cover her ears. Ping makes a break for it. Pong gallops after him, dragging me along. I drop my leash, too.

The dogs head for the shortcut between the park and the street. Where the path meets the street, the dogs know better than to cross the road. Smart — that keeps them safe. But it also means they turn left and charge toward my house instead of the Bennetts'. Renée catches up to me.

A few people have decorated for Halloween already but the dogs dash past the bloated straw zombies and assorted tombstones, not even giving them a leg lift. They get to my house way ahead of us. Renée and I are not champion marathon runners.

Lightning zigzags across the sky and another rumble ends with a crack.

"We're not supposed to bring them in. Mom's allergies, remember?" I tell Renée.

"I'm not going one step further," Renée answers. Her sparkly red glasses could use windshield wipers. Her dark hair lies plastered to her scalp. Water drips from her nose. Her uniform clings wet to her, a shade darker than its usual pale khaki.

Ping grumbles and shifts on his paws. Then he jumps up and does a *scratch, scratch* at the door, ending his grumble in a high-pitched yowl. I unlock it and push it open.

"Dad ... Dad? ... Dad!" No answer. I flip the switch but nothing happens. No light. No Dad.

"Power's out." Renée steps in behind me. The dogs push in around us.

Lightning cracks so close the house shudders. The dogs scatter, shaking themselves as they run.

A phone rings from the kitchen. I look at Renée and she shakes her head. "Have you not seen that episode of *Mythbusters*? You're never supposed to answer a landline during a thunderstorm."

Still Renée follows me to the kitchen. I take a deep breath as we both stare at the phone. The caller ID says *Unknown*. But besides telemarketers, Mom's the only one who calls on the landline. She's a flight attendant, away on another of her three-day jaunts. This call could be the only chance I get to talk to her.

I pick up.

"Hi, Stephen." It *is* my mom. "This is an emergency. Have to talk fast."

Answering the phone turns out to be my first mistake of the day. I wanted a story from her. Something funny. Maybe about how rare lightning strikes are. Funny stories are what she usually gives me when I am anxious, and then we laugh together. I miss her laugh when she's away.

Mom continues. "Flights are delayed due to extreme weather conditions and a passenger is hysterical here."

I so don't need an emergency to deal with right now. Dad's out there somewhere in this storm. There's no power and I shouldn't even be holding anything connected by wire to a source of electricity.

Mom's still talking: "Coincidentally, she's the neighbour who moved into that corner house on Overton and Cavendish a couple months ago. The house flipper with the big dumpster in her drive-way. She needs someone to check on her pet."

Crackle, crackle.

I take a deep breath. In … out …

Unless I get electrocuted, answering the phone may be just a tiny boo-boo, after all. Dad tells me all the time that mistakes are literally "missed takes," sort of little rehearsals that don't go quite right. If you practise enough, some of the misses actually do "take." So I count mine and live in hope.

"The address is —"

Crackle, crackle.

"Overton. The key is under the second pot from the front door. She's worried about King eating —"

Mom seems almost finished when —

CRACK!

I drop the phone.

DAY ONE, MISTAKE TWO

"Did you get burnt?" Renée asks.

"No. I let go just in case."

"'Cause when Attila put his tongue to the bug zapper, he said it felt like burning."

"No burning." I don't even ask about why her brother licked a bug zapper. It's just the kind of thing he would do, probably for an art experience. Instead, I pick up the phone and listen, but, of course, Mom is gone. "I need to go back out."

A siren warbles in the distance. A fire? An accident? Or maybe someone else wasn't so lucky answering the phone when lightning struck.

Renée peers through the kitchen window. It's a charcoal-grey square. Thunder rumbles and she runs to the door, presses her back against it, and throws her arms and legs out in a jumping jack to block the way. "You're not leaving us alone!"

Renée has a thing about being by herself in a house, even in good weather.

"I'm supposed to make sure King is fed. You can come, too." I step closer but she doesn't budge.

"Whoever King is, he can wait till the storm ends."

"A new customer." She knows how badly we need those. Dad makes dog treats, and lately he's even been knitting dog sweaters to help boost business.

"So what!" Renée rolls her eyes. "You won't be able to feed the dog if you're zapped to a crisp on the way."

Another rumble and crack shakes the house. I shudder. "You're right. Ping? Pong?" I call out. "Where'd they disappear to?"

"I don't know. But I have to go to the bathroom. Do you have a flashlight?"

"Downstairs, plugged in near Dad's workbench."

The door to the basement is open and we both peer down the dark tunnel that is, of course, windowless.

"Fine," she says. "Might as well use the bathroom down there as well." Renée gropes blindly down the stairs to the bathroom, which will be even darker.

After I hear Renée shout, "Found the flashlight," I head for the large picture window in the family room. Exactly where you're not supposed to stand during a bad storm. Imagine if the glass shatters. I watch mesmerized. Leaves must be blocking the sewer drains, 'cause a river runs along the curb. The rain punches little pockmarks on the water.

A narrow white panel truck whooshes through, making waves like a motorboat. The truck has a tall cab. Weird looking but I've seen it before. *Diamond Drywall*. Seems like lots of houses around here need new walls.

Renée screams.

"What! What?" I dash down in the darkness.

The bathroom door flings open. "I found Ping." In the dull flashlight beam, I can barely make out her silhouette. Something wriggles in her arms. "Behind the toilet." She snorts. "Thought he was a rat."

I giggle. Renée sneezes.

"Gesundheit," I say.

"Thanks. Do you have a sweatshirt I can borrow?"

"Sure." I take the flashlight and lead her to the laundry room next door where I sort through some old clothes in the cupboard, shining the beam on each top till I find the one I want. It's probably the only one small enough, a red shirt that Grandma bought me four years ago. *Boy Genius* it reads across the front. Never could part with it. I toss it to her.

Ping follows Renée back into the bathroom, where she changes. Meanwhile, I switch from my wet shirt to another favourite, this time from the clean basket, the only one there that's mine. It's a navy-blue sweatshirt with the words *Keep Calm and Walk the Dog* across it.

"Do they have this in Girl?" Renée asks as she steps out.

"They should. I know there's one that says *Little Princess.*"

"*Princess Genius,* that's what I'd like."

"Fits, anyway." Princess Genius would be perfect for Renée, too. In her spare time, she studies Wikipedia.

Ping at our heels, we head up to the family room to watch the storm. When the world lights up with another crack, I see a familiar figure in a hood heading up the walkway. Finally! Dad's home.

But instead of feet, he appears to have a sea of wet rats moving him along. I gulp, and Ping leaps out of Renée's arms. He lands running and barking.

The door opens and Dad appears. "I brought the Yorkies."

Raff, raff, raff, raff, raff!

The sea of wet rats rushes in, barking. Suddenly, the room fills with that certain smell, musty yet sweet, with a tang of dirt to it. Wet dog. I love it. "I didn't think they could stay alone in the storm," Dad says.

"Great minds think alike." Renée nods as Ping sniffs one of the gang.

This could be a mistake — number two — and a big one. The Yorkies don't even get along with each other, never mind with Ping and Pong.

"Where's Pong?" Dad asks.

I shrug. "Somewhere in the house."

The wet dogs begin shaking the water from their fur. Dad sighs. "Can you help me towel these guys off?"

"Sure." I head to the kitchen broom closet where we keep our rags, Renée following so close that I swear I can feel her breath against my back. The door hangs wide open. Odd. I hand her the flash-light so I can reach for the rags on the top shelf.

Suddenly, something flaps against me from below. I leap back, knocking Renée over. "Pong!" I cry and his tail slaps the floor harder.

Renée scrambles up. "I'm okay." She shines the flashlight so we can see the skinny black and white dog stuffed in the small space with the broom and vacuum cleaner.

"It's all right, Pong. Lightning can't strike you inside the house." With the spotlight on him, he drops his snout open into a kind of grin-pant. He looks embarrassed but he still doesn't come out.

I reach up again and pull down a bunch of faded towels. "Here!" I pitch a few to Renée and we find our way back to the family room. I throw Dad some towels and we each tackle a dog. I dry off Hunter, that's what his tag says. Hunter as in green. All five Yorkies are named for colours of the rainbow, and Dad's knitting them sweaters in their colours. Mrs. Irwin, their owner, is an artist like Mr. Kowalski. They used to work together at Mohawk College.

"You're such a good, good girl, Rose," Renée tells an identical Yorkie as she scrubs her.

The other couple of Yorkies tear around the room rubbing their bodies against the couch and the carpet. Ping chases them.

"Your mother's going to be so stuffed up." Dad shakes his head as he wipes off another dog. "So much dog dander flying around. We're going to have to steam clean the carpet and chairs."

"Why don't we herd all the animals down to the basement?" I suggest.

"Great idea! And Renée, tell your mother where you are."

"Already texted her," she answers. "C'mon, Rose. Ping."

I open the door to the basement. "Here boy," I call to Hunter, holding out a liver bite.

Dad shoos the other Yorkies down with us. "Go. Blue, Goldie, Violet." He snaps his finger after each colour.

We head downstairs.

Renée holds the flashlight, which produces a single beam of light in a black pit full of restless fur. When Renée shifts the beam to find the couch, the dogs hurl themselves after it. She shifts the beam so I can find my way and they chase it again. Pong gallops down the stairs to join the pack. Seven dogs now. One of the Yorkies falls onto another, and they tumble and snap and snarl at each other. Ping barks — the referee.

"Stop it!" Renée orders as she shuts the flashlight.

A few more growls and they do. She sets the light on its tail end in the middle of the coffee table and turns it back on.

Too much wet-dog smell gags me. I sneeze.

A couple of the Yorkies perform a duo whine.

Which reminds me: "I wonder how poor King feels?" I picture some puppy shaking and whimpering in a crate all by himself.

As if to warn us, another siren warbles at that moment.

"It's nothing," Renée says. "Don't worry. Street lights are out. Lots of fender benders."

"Still. As soon as the rain stops, I'm going to check on him."

But the storm goes on for hours. Dad brings us a battery-operated lantern and the three of us play Renée's even crazier version of Crazy Eights, where all kinds of cards become wild. The game drags on till every dog falls asleep, many of them snoring. Dad nods off, too. I cover him with a sleeping bag. With Ping's head on her lap, Renée slaps down a Jack. "Miss a turn."

"You win. Honestly. I'm going upstairs to see what's happening." Out of habit, I flip a light switch but nothing happens. I tramp up the stairs, shutting the door behind me so the dogs stay in the basement. I head for the family room and stare out the window.

"Thanks for closing the door on me." Renée joins me at the window.

"Sorry." I glance her way but she's smiling. "I think it's letting up," I say hopefully.

"No more lightning, anyway," Renée says.

"I have to visit King."

"Really?"

"Mom said it was an emergency."

The real second mistake of the day. And it's a doozy. I should have told Dad about King as soon as he stepped through the door. He would have driven over and checked on him immediately. Maybe he'd have gotten a little wet, but it's that kind of dedication that his clients count on. Instead, we throw on our jackets, still soggy from the first downpour, and leave Ping and Pong behind. I figure if I can check on King and everything's all right, I can present Dad with the information afterward. Knowing Dad won't hear me anyway, I cover all my bases by calling, "We're going out to check on a new client." Then we head out to help a pet we've never met before.

DAY ONE, MISTAKE THREE

We pass Renée's brother, Attila, and his sometimes girlfriend, Star, on the way out. Attila's not a tough-guy nickname or anything, it's a common name in Hungary where their parents are from. Still, he can be scary. He's tall, with a mohawk sprouting from his head and muscles rippling against the sleeves of his torn black sweater. Today he carries a brown saddlebag over his shoulder, maybe to carry his spray paints — he's a graffiti artist. That brown bag provides the only touch of colour against all his black clothes.

Star's wearing a couple of nose rings and her classic skull-and-crossbones leggings with a black leather jacket and mini skirt. The all-black artist look, too. Nice to see her nose all healed up. Ping, in an enthusiastic jump and lick, accidentally caught her stud with his teeth a couple of weeks ago.

Attila and Star both hold cell phones in front of their faces. Are they taking some kind of strange selfies or photos of houses? They don't seem the Pokémon-hunting type.

"Hi," Renée calls to her brother.

Not taking his eyes from the little screen, he grunts.

"Hey," I say to Star.

She smiles back. Slyly, I think, but I'll never trust her. Star and Attila stole some Halloween displays, a mailbox, and a garden gnome for an art instal-lation. While everything came out all right in the end, she threatened to tell Animal Control about Ping tearing her nose if we reported her.

"Over there! A serpent!" She calls out, and she and Attila cross the street.

A large green Cadillac brakes. A voice like a can-non shoots from the car.

"You stupid kids. Can't you ever put your cell phones down?" Mr. Rupert yells. He lives close to Renée and Attila and must be out on bail. He was arrested for carrying a weapon a couple of weeks ago.

Star smiles and waves a finger, friendly-style, even though it's not a polite gesture.

The Cadillac fishtails away. *Support Our Troops*, the bumper sticker reads.

"Stupid cell phone, anyway," Attila says. He pulls his arm back as if to hurl it.

Star grabs his arm. "The app crashed, still in development, remember?" She plucks the cell phone from his hands and shakes her head. "Way better than catching Pokémon. Just have to tell the developer where it went wrong."

"Stupid Rupert!" Attila grumbles.

We continue on. "If I were them, I wouldn't mess with Mr. Rupert," I tell Renée. The mailbox they stole for their entry in the Burlington Art Gallery contest was the last mailbox Mrs. Rupert made before she died. High sentimental value for Mr. Rupert.

"Could he change his mind and still press charges on the mailbox thing?" Renée asks. Mr. Rupert found out at the gallery reception that Star and Attila had taken it. But when their installation tied for first place in popular choice, he forgave the theft.

"No, he likes seeing his wife's work in the gallery. Still, you don't mess with him; he's always ready to explode." Renée has seen him prowling around in his military fatigues like he's looking for more reasons to be angry. Who knows what will set him off.

We keep strolling. Up ahead is the new client's house. Easy to spot: the huge green bin in the driveway holds a sky-high pile of broken wallboard.

"Mom said they were house flippers," I tell Renée. "But this house looks like something broke when it flipped."

I turn down the walkway and head for a row of purple winter cabbages in pots near the house.

"Haven't you ever watched that show?" Renée asks. "Where flippers buy homes and sell them for much higher prices after they've renovated them?"

"Can't say I have."

I pull the key out from under the second pot.

"Hey, Stephen, what's up?" A bicycle wobbles by. It's Red, a grade seven guy from school with a skateboard tucked under one arm.

"Nothing much," I answer, but he's not around anymore for the answer. I unlock the door.

No barking. That's strange. King's not a great watchdog, that's for sure. "Do you think the dog's deaf or something?"

Renée shrugs and we step in. Still no puppy greeting or growling at us. "Did your mom say where King likes to hang out?"

I shake my head. We look around. There's a fine

layer of white dust everywhere in the front room, especially over the floor. No paw prints, though.

The wall between this living area and the kitchen has been knocked out — accounts for the stuff in the driveway bin. "Most dogs hate thunderstorms," I say. "He's probably hiding. I'll check the first bedroom, you go for the second." I walk through a hallway and turn into a big bedroom that looks crazy messy. Drawers gape open with clothes hanging out like they're trying to escape. The mattress of the bed lies bare, the sheets and duvet tangled on the floor. I peek under the bed. Just a pizza box with crusts. Clearly, no dog has ever been here or they'd be eaten.

I head for the next door off the hallway, which opens to a large bathroom complete with a big Jacuzzi tub. I look behind the toilet. Nothing. Inside the cupboard, just in case. Toilet paper and cleaners.

"Nooooo! Stephen, come quick!"

I run toward Renée's voice. Turns out it's coming from a family room at the back of the house. She's standing in front of a large aquarium, cradling a limp white mouse. On the floor is the wire mesh cover.

"He's so cold," Renée whimpers as she strokes the mouse with one finger. "Poor little guy."

I reach over and touch him, too. "That's strange. He's dripping." I look up at the ceiling. "The roof's not leaking."

"Check out the aquarium," Renée says. "Not a single pellet of food."

I stare at it, thinking. There's a bowl of water, wood chips, and a tree branch in the aquarium. A big lamp hangs over it. As we stand there looking at the aquarium, the light comes on. "Power's back." I reach my hand under the lamp. "It's a warming light."

"Aww! This is all my fault. You should have come here hours ago. He might not have frozen to death."

He's cold, he's dripping … things add up for me slowly. "This mouse is defrosting!"

"I know. You could have come and given him a blanket or something … wait a minute, it's not *that* cold. Not even outside."

"Exactly," I answer. Mistake number three of the day is pet-identity confusion. First we assumed King was a dog, then a rodent. "This mouse isn't King," I tell Renée. "This mouse is King's dinner!"

DAY ONE, MISTAKE FOUR

Renée gently places the dead mouse down on the woodchips in the aquarium. Then she turns to me. "So if King eats mice, that means he's a … a …"

"Snake!" I finish her sentence.

Her eyes get big, like little moons in her face — a

thing they always do when she's shocked. We both jump on the couch.

"What kind of snake, do you think?"

"Well, it's not a vegetarian." Feeling a little silly, I drop down to my knees and look under the couch. Dust bunnies. I climb down onto the floor and check under the entertainment unit. A *Star Trek* DVD.

"What's the owner going to say?"

"Nothing. Nobody has to know. 'Cause we're going to find him." I lift a couch cushion. Immediately, Renée leaps down.

Under cushion number one, I find a quarter, which I put on the coffee table.

Renée squints as she peers around the room. "Supposing we do spot him, how do we catch him?"

I stop searching for a moment to think on this. "With our bare hands. Haven't you ever been to a reptile show?"

"Sure. With the class last year at the Royal Botanical Gardens, same as you."

"Did you line up to touch the snake?" I start looking again. Under cushion number two, I find a nail and a business card: *McCains, Sell Homes Sooner*. I put those on the table, too.

"That snake was just a tiny garter." Her voice sounds frowny.

"You didn't line up, did you?"

Renée shakes her head. "Now my brother, Attila, he let some reptile dude drape a constrictor on his shoulders …" She shudders. "I just couldn't."

"Yeah, well, me either. I like animals with fur and feet — four, tops. No tarantulas." Under cushion three, I find a beer bottle cap and a pamphlet about ball pythons. I hold it up for Renée to see. "I think we just found out what kind of snake we're looking for." I skim the information. "According to this, they make great pets, can be picky eaters, and are escape artists."

"Sounds like King, all right. And seeing as he left the mouse …" She jumps back on the couch. "He must still be hungry."

"I don't think he's anywhere in this room. I already searched the bathroom."

"Yes. But that was when you thought you were looking for a dog. I read a book last summer called *Snake in My Toilet.*"

"Oh my gosh, so did I!"

Renée follows me to the bathroom, where I carefully lift the toilet lid. Nothing.

My phone buzzes, then. I pull it from my pocket and read a text from Dad. *Where are you? Come home and have some lunch.*

I'm not going to tell him about King just yet. Instead, I thumb-type back to him. *Had an emergency. On my way back now.*

He sends another message, and as I read it, I can't help myself. "Uh-oh!"

"What? What?" Renée asks.

"Take a look."

Renée reads out loud. *Be careful to lock the Bennetts' house when you return Ping and Pong. Mrs. Irwin's home was broken into.* She looks up. "The Yorkies' house? That's not good!"

"I hope Mrs. Irwin's not blaming Dad."

"You think the Yorkies would have prevented the break-in?" Renée asks.

"Or the burglar could have killed them," I answer.

"They *are* annoying," she agrees. "Quite possibly, your dad saved them."

"Probably. C'mon. Let's go home and eat."

"Hey, maybe we can come back with the dogs and they can sniff out the snake!"

"If the owner just flew out, we should have enough time to get King back." I kneel down, lift a heating vent, and squint.

"Anything?"

"Can't really see. I remember from the book that snakes like warm pipes. But the heater's not on yet."

"Let's go!" Renée says, and I follow her out the door.

Carefully, I turn the key and jiggle the door handle to make sure the door is locked. Then I place the key under the second flowerpot again. Behind me I hear whistling.

"Hey, Mr. Ron!" Renée calls out.

"Hi," I call, too. It's our old crossing guard, turned bricklayer since he drove a Volkswagen beetle into our school. Without his orange vest and hat, he looks different, smaller, less hair maybe, but his belly still leads the way as he strolls forward. The big surprise is that he's walking Bailey, a golden retriever who belongs to Mr. Mason, one of Dad's clients.

"Hi, kids," he says. His face turns pink.

We don't ask him about the dog, but he explains, anyway.

"Just doing a favour for the boss."

"That's nice of you," I tell him. *Client stealer.* As we join them on the sidewalk, Bailey wags like crazy and nudges us for a pat. I drop down and rub his head. Bailey, a big fan of Dad's liver bites, licks hungrily at my pocket.

"So, you're taking a break from a job?" Renée asks. She always chats up adults, asking them questions that are really none of her business.

Mr. Ron frowns. "Not enough brick work for both of us." He points at me. "Say, if your dad ever needs another dog walker, I'm great with animals. Had plenty of experience walking kids, after all. Twenty years of it."

"I'll tell him. Thanks." Even if we had tons of clients and needed more help, I'm not sure Dad would trust him anymore, since he drove that car into our school.

"Good. Well, gotta go." Mr. Ron tugs Bailey on and raises his big stop-sign-sized hand. "Bye."

"So long."

"Darn," I tell Renée after he leaves. "Mr. Mason never likes to spend money on dog walking. If he can get Mr. Ron to do it for him for free, we'll lose Bailey for sure."

We continue down the block, the sun shining now. A few trees still spit rain on us as we pass under them.

A skateboarder glides and swoops side to side across Cavendish. It's Principal Watier's son. Trust him to skate as though he owns the road. Doesn't he know this is a bus route? Usually, he skates angry, leaping and crashing and swearing. The dogs bark a warning whenever he's nearby. But today he's fast and graceful and doesn't even notice us without Ping and Pong. Skating more slowly behind him is Red, biting his lip and waving his hands for balance. He doesn't see us, either, he's concentrating that hard.

"Look over there!" Renée points in an entirely different direction. "In the sky over Brant Hills. It's a double rainbow!"

"Wow." We both stop and stare. "Funny, it arcs down right near Mrs. Irwin's house."

"Maybe that's where she got her idea for naming the Yorkies," Renée suggests.

"Wonder what got stolen. Her pot of gold?"

"Maybe some art," Renée suggests as we start walking again.

We make it home just as Dad heads out on his way with the five furballs. They look way better now. Dry and happy, none of them fighting. "Did you blow-dry their hair, Dad?"

He nods. "Wanted them to look extra nice." One is wearing a green sweater.

"Well, they sure do!"

"So you finished knitting Hunter's sweater?" Renée asks as she stoops to pat him. "That's record time." The other Yorkies crowd around her.

"Yes. Once I heard about the robbery, I knit like crazy to finish it."

"Fits perfectly. Looks good on him." I drop down and scratch at another Yorkie's ears. "Mrs. Irwin will be happy."

Dad shakes his head and frowns. "I don't think so."

Another Yorkie slurps at my face. I squeeze my eyes closed "You're right. How can you be happy if you've just been robbed. A mistake to even suggest it." Number four, if I'm counting.

Dad waves his hand in the air as if shooing my thought away. "The biggest mistake is mine. Mrs. Irwin claims I left her door unlocked." Dad closes his eyes for a moment and sighs. "She fired me."

DAY ONE, MISTAKE FIVE

"*Did* you forget, Dad?" I push the slurpy Yorkie away from my face and pat it. Another Yorkie flips on its back for a belly rub.

"No, I don't think so. I'm almost positive I locked it. But the police say there was no sign of forced entry and the door was open."

"You jiggled the handle to make sure the key worked, like you showed me?" I pat one dog with one hand and rub another's belly with the other.

"Pretty sure I did." Dad's face looks red. "I can almost see myself doing it."

"Even if you didn't, it doesn't mean the robbery's your fault," Renée says. The other Yorkies crowd around her for pats, too. So many of them.

"Doesn't Mrs. Irwin have an alarm system?" I ask.

"Yes. And like everyone else's, it was going off because of the power failure. No one ever pays attention anymore."

Renée nods. "No one checks on cars when alarms go off, either. They're just annoying."

Dad shakes his head, looking annoyed with himself. "Usually, I talk to myself as I lock the door. Trick I learned in air traffic. That way, what you're doing becomes less mindless. You register that you're doing it. But I must have made a mistake."

"You tell me all the time that mistakes are good things. They help us discover amazing stuff. Is that only true for kids? Not for adults?"

"No, I believe we're all meant to make mistakes. They teach us things." Dad runs his hand through his hair and frowns. "Losing Mrs. Irwin is like losing five clients. Maybe what I'm supposed to learn is that dog walking is not for me."

"You love it, though!" Renée says.

Dad shrugs. "Yes, well. We have to pay the bills like everyone else."

Hunter licks at another Yorkie's mouth. Then that little mop rat rumbles low and cranky.

"What did the robbers take? Her paintings?" I ask.

The Yorkie rumbling grows into a growl.

"No. It was a Mr. Universe gold medal."

"The one Mr. Sawyer won before he became custodian?" Renée asks.

"That's the one." Dad reels the Yorkies closer. "Mrs. Irwin was creating a special display for it. A bust of him."

I try to picture that for a moment. Mr. Sawyer has long blond hair and a strong face, but what I best remember him for is accidentally-on-purpose tripping kids with his broom when they forgot to wipe their boots on the mat.

The Yorkie growl turns into a teeth-bared snarl.

"Stop it, Rose!" Dad commands the dog as he gives the leash a shake. Instantly, the growling stops.

"You're so good with them," Renée says. "She'll hire you back, Mr. Noble. Don't you worry. This is Mrs. Irwin's mistake."

"Yeah," I agree. "No one else will want to walk these guys."

"You've got a point." Dad's face brightens for a moment. He reaches into his pocket for treats, and all the dogs immediately sit, ears up. He smiles, then sighs as he doles out the liver bites. "For now I just hope she still pays for all the sweaters. I'm out for the wool, at least."

Satisfied with their treats, the Yorkies jump up on their paws again and tug at their leashes.

"Okay, well, bologna's in the fridge. Make yourself something to eat. See you later." Dad walks off, looking a little happier than before.

Once he and the Yorkies are gone, we can hear Ping barking, see his little head through the glass window in our door. Pong's long narrow snout and round black eyes hang over him. "Dad didn't keep them in the basement."

"Guess his mind is elsewhere," Renée says as I unlock the door. "Okay, I'm starving. Let's eat."

"Me too," I agree.

Ping bounces up to greet Renée, yipping frantically. Pong bumps silently against my leg. I pat his head. When Ping yips my way, I crouch down and pat him, too, except then he jumps up and licks inside my nostril. I push his muzzle away gently. Even while wiping away dog spit, I love this. Love having someone so happy that we've arrived. I will hate it if Dad gives up his dog-walking business. All because of Mrs. Irwin. An artist who didn't even believe in art until the art gallery contest.

Once we give the dogs some love, we all head for the kitchen. I grab some bologna and some bread. "How would anyone know the Mr. Universe medal was at Mrs. Irwin's house?" I wonder out loud as I spread mustard on my slices of bread.

Renée puts peanut butter on one of hers while toasting the other. "Maybe they didn't. They just saw it in her studio or wherever she's creating the sculpture. I've heard that the medal has a lot of gold in it." The toast pops and she adds a dab of ketchup before slapping the bread slices together.

Yuck, I know, right? But it's not as bad as it sounds. I nuke mine a little — I like my bologna warm — and grab for the peanut butter, too. "Wonder if Mr. Sawyer has insurance for the medal."

"You would think so," Renée answers. "But money can't replace something like that."

I roll up a slice of bologna and both the dogs sit pretty. I toss off a small bit to Ping and the rest to

Pong. After I pour Renée and me a couple glasses of milk, we sit down to eat, dogs at our feet.

The landline rings.

Rouf, rouf! Ping sounds a second alarm.

There's no reason for me not to answer it this time. I'm always polite to telemarketers because Dad says that could be his next job. But I read the name in the little phone window. *Mason Man.* Bailey's owner, Dad's sometimes client. Builder of all things brick and mortar. He fixed our school wall after Mr. Ron drove into it with the Volkswagen.

"Hello, Stephen Noble speaking."

"Where's your father?" a gravelly voice asks.

"Hi, Mr. Mason. He's out with clients. Why don't you try his business number?"

"I did. He's not picking up."

"May I take a message for him?"

"Yeah. I want my house key back. My phone and laptop were stolen and all my doors and windows were locked."

"My dad always loses his phone around the house. Sometimes under newspapers ..."

"Yeah. Well, mine are both red, so I can find them real easy. And I always keep the laptop in my office."

"Oh!" That's all I can say for a moment. My next line should have just been, "I'll pass on your message as soon as he gets in." Instead, I can't help myself. Mistake number five of the day makes me sound as though I think he's considering Dad as his thief. As though I have to defend him.

I ask, "Were you away from your home during the storm?"

"Yeah."

"My dad and I and Renée — we were all in the basement playing cards. By flashlight," I add as if this detail makes it sound more truthful.

"Well, he can tell all that to the cops. In the meantime, just tell him I want my key."

DAY ONE, MISTAKE SIX

"Dad can't have forgotten to lock two doors," I tell Renée after I hang up.

Renée finishes the last bite of her sandwich. "Never, not your dad. Why?"

"Mr. Mason says he was robbed, too. No sign of forced entry there, either."

"Same MO, eh?" She licks a drop of ketchup from her thumb.

"I guess. What does that even mean?"

"*Modus operandi.* Latin for method of operation." Trust Renée to know that. She loves to hang out at the library and just google stuff. "He's not that great a customer, anyway. So who cares."

"True, but he said something about the police. If they suspect Dad and it gets around, who will want to hire him?"

"People who know him," Renée answers. "I would hire him."

"You don't have a pet."

"Someday. I'm working on my dad."

She can work all she wants, but Mr. Kobai is one of those neat freak guys with ironed jeans — sort of like his son, Attila, except for way less hair and they don't get along at all. I can't see him allowing an animal in the house. He can barely stand Attila, and his bedroom is in the basement. I text Dad about Mr. Mason.

"You know what we have to do," Renée tells me, and I know the answer before it comes out of her mouth.

"Find the thief to prove my dad is innocent."

"Uh-huh. Not sure how yet, but it will come to me," Renée says.

Waiting for ideas is uncomfortable. I stare at the kitchen phone. "I wish Mom would call back so she could tell us when King's owners are coming home."

"Regardless, we have to try at least one more time to find King."

"With the dogs? What if someone sees us?"

"No one will care. King might be back in his aquarium, and all we have to do is put the lid on. With some kind of weight on top of the lid this time."

"You're right." Renée's always right. "C'mon, Pong. Let's go, Ping."

We leash them up and head around the block again. The air feels less sticky, more fall-like, only with no bite yet. Perfect dog-walking weather. Back to their normal selves, Ping and Pong pull us like a wagon. We pass the clumsy skateboarder, Red, who's walking his Pomeranian, a strange little animal with stick-out orangey-red fur. They say dogs and their owners look alike; well, those two certainly do. Besides the colouring, they both have the same startled resting-face look.

"Let's cross the street," I tell Renée when I see a lady in a neon, lime-green sweatsuit jogging with her Rottweiler. It's not because her outfit is blinding; her dog Buddy snapped at Pong once. One-quarter Buddy's size, Ping still wanted to kill him. Ping can give Pong a hard time, but he never lets anyone else do the same. The jogging lady believes in letting dogs work things out; Noble Dog Walking does not.

But she calls after me when I'm halfway across. "Hey. Do you mind giving me a business card? I just won another contract. Cleaning for a whole real estate branch. I could use your dad's service again."

"Renée, take Pong for a second." I hand her his leash. Then I fumble for a Noble Dog Walking card from my pocket and cross back. "We actually have a couple of time slots opening up," I say as I give her the card.

She holds it up. "You should have these made into fridge magnets."

"Just put us on speed dial!" Renée calls with a friendly smile. I like her speed dial idea.

Buddy's stubby propeller tail winds up, like he's all happy. Under his breath, though, he's rumbling.

"Buddy likes you, that's nice," his owner says and pats his massive black and brown head. "He loves your dad, too."

Sure he does. I flip him a liver bite and the rumbling stops. Buddy snaps it up and then opens his snout into a panting grin, shakes his head, and lands drool on my hand. "Better call soon." I wipe my hand on my pants. "All the dogs want Dad. He gets booked up fast."

"Okay," she says and the two of them jog away.

We continue on to King's house. I grab the key from under the flowerpot near the walkway and open the door.

"I wonder. What can we give them to sniff?" Renée asks herself out loud.

"Nothing. They're not bloodhounds."

She doesn't listen to me. Last week she gave them a knitted cap to smell and they led us to Star, the cap's owner. Probably a lucky coincidence. "C'mon, Ping." She snaps her fingers at him.

Pong and I follow her to the back of the house where the aquarium sits complete with a thawed, soggy mouse and wood chips. She scoops up a handful of chips. "This might have some of King's scent on it." She lowers her hand to Ping's head and he licks some up.

Ack, ack, ack. He horks it back up.

"Let's just take them from room to room, and see where they go," I suggest.

"Okay."

We guide them to the master bedroom. Renée immediately drops the leash and Ping tears around sniffing.

"You think you should let him loose?"

"No worries. He'll bark his head off if he finds King."

The dogs both seem excited, running from corner to corner as if they're on to something. Ping dives under the bare bed and scores the pizza crusts. Pong joins him.

After their snack, no smells call to them anymore.

We grab their leashes and take them to the bathroom. *Sniff, sniff,* nothing. Into the second bedroom, which is more like an exercise room. Some weights are piled up on a rack against a wall, and a stationary bike and treadmill face a shelf with a TV on it. Ping continues to sniff. Again nothing.

The last bedroom is full of boxes. *Sniff, sniff, sniff, sniff.* No python slithers out from anywhere. Maybe I'm even relieved.

We head down the stairs into the basement, which is just four walls of cinderblock. More boxes. We guide them to pipes we think might be warm.

"Let's face it. That python could be anywhere," I tell Renée. "We need to catch a break. A really lucky one."

But, no break for us. Not a trace of snake anywhere. We head back upstairs.

"Okay. What the heck, set them loose and let them go where they like." I drop Pong's leash, and Renée sets Ping free. Both gallop to the kitchen.

Ping suddenly barks his high-pitched excited bark. Pong lets go a loud woof that sounds deep and dangerous. And he rarely makes a sound.

Could it be? Renée and I look at each other for a moment and then slowly, step by step, head toward the barking.

"Ball pythons are small," Renée reminds me. "They're friendly, too, otherwise no one would have them as pets."

When we finally make it into the kitchen, the dogs are both lying on the floor in front of the fridge, chowing down on something.

One of the doors is wide open: the freezer. I'm sure it wasn't like that when we came in before. We would have noticed. Neither Ping nor Pong has opposable thumbs so I'm guessing someone left it open, just a little, and the dogs pawed it open the rest of the way once the smell of food kicked in.

Okay, well, letting them run loose was definitely mistake number six.

"Ew, ew, ew!" Renée hops from one foot to the other. "They're eating mice!"

DAY ONE, MISTAKE SEVEN

"Give me that!" I grab the frozen mouse from Pong — he's chewed through the plastic wrap already. When I put the little stiff back in the freezer, I see a stack of bodies on the bottom shelf. King's food supply?

Meanwhile, Renée struggles to get Ping's away from him. He thinks it a game and dodges from side to side, growling.

Renée grabs onto one end of the mouse as Ping shakes the other. "Gross, gross, gross!" Her whole arm shakes along. "LET GO, Ping!" Renée's losing it.

What's even more gross is that the owners keep their frozen pizza and a couple of steaks one shelf up from the mice. "Oh. What's this?" Next to the pile of steaks, I spot a silver bell about the size of a small fist.

Renée finally forces the mouse out from between Ping's teeth. "Uh!" She squeezes in beside me and throws it into the bottom of the freezer.

"Look at that!" I point to the silver bell. The dogs move in close, trying to get around us for more mouse sushi. "Leave it!" I nudge them away with my foot.

Renée can't resist a shiny thing. She pulls it off the shelf and smiles. "This is an engagement ring box. See?" She lifts the lid. Inside is a blue velvet cushion with a slot. She sticks her finger in it. "This is where the diamond ring usually goes."

Ping and Pong sit pretty now in eternal hope that she holds a treat.

"Why would anyone keep an empty ring box in the freezer?"

"My mom always hides her expensive jewellery in the freezer when we go away." Renée hands the silver bell back and shuts the door.

"But the box is empty!" My voice rises just enough so that Ping must think we're arguing. He warns me with a bark, startling Renée for a second.

She does a two-step back and nearly falls. "Ick, ick!" She points to the puddle on the floor, then gives the dogs a hard stare. "Pong? Ping?"

Ears up, they stare innocently back at her.

"Don't blame them. The water looks clear."

Ping barks again as if in agreement. Pong slumps down and looks away.

"If it really isn't dog pee," Renée says, "the door must have been open awhile. The freezer must have been leaking."

Ping sneaks in closer and laps at the puddle.

"See, that proves it," I say. "No way would he drink his own pee. We just didn't notice the

water before." I think some more as I put the
bell-shaped box back in the freezer. "Engagement
rings have diamonds. They're valuable, right? You
don't think the ring that belonged in that bell was
stolen, do you?"

Renée shrugs. "Most people wear their engagement rings twenty-four seven. Hard to tell
if someone broke in here or not, with the mess."
Renée sweeps Ping away from the fridge with her
foot. He pounces on her leg, ready to play. "Stop!"
she tells him. Then turns to me. "But honestly,
who leaves their freezer open?"

"Actually, once when I stuffed the ice cream con-
tainer in, the lid fell off and wedged itself between
the door and the rest of the freezer."

"All right, but what kind of slob leaves all their
drawers open?"

My cheeks get hot. "Sometimes, when I'm late
for school and trying to find something …"

"Oh, come on, Stephen. So why are the sheets off
the bed?"

"Someone meant to change them. Then the phone
rang in the middle. Someone catching a plane?"

"Or … someone looking for something.
Valuables." Renée clasps her hands together and
grins. "Maybe someone even stole King. Pythons
are exotic animals. They must be worth something."

I shake my head at her.

Her smile drops a little. "Why not? Don't you see, that will get us off the hook for not checking in on him sooner. And … we won't have to pick him up with our bare hands."

"Another robbery with no sign of a break-in. Where Noble Dog Walkers have access to a key? Not only will we lose all our customers, we'll get arrested."

"Never thought of it that way." She bunches up her mouth and then brightens. "Okay, okay. I have an idea."

It's a long, long walk to the Burlington Animal Shelter. Renée ends up carrying Ping the last block. As we draw closer to the building, other dogs begin barking, deep, throaty big-dog barks.

Ping finds his energy again, leaps down, and yaps back. As we step through the doors, Pong perks up, too. It's a school office–type beige room with a standard bulletin board full of posters near the door. Cages line the walls. All boring except for the soft mews and chirps that raise the dogs' ears in alert. The smell of cat, dog, cedar chips, and disinfectant captures both Pong and Ping's nostrils in a quiver of delight. They pull in every direction.

I steer Pong to the large U-shaped counter where a woman sits, chin in her hand, staring at a computer. She looks familiar, strong-looking with curly golden hair.

"Excuse me, Miss ..." I begin.

She looks up. "Hi, how are you. Looking for a cat today? We have lots."

"No, um," I start. Her voice sounds familiar.

"Do you know about our Cat-astrophe coming up this Monday? All cats will be marked down."

Renée jumps in. "You're the lady with that great wall hanging of the church. You entered it in the art contest!"

I snap my fingers as I remember her name. "Janet Lacey."

"That's right. And you're the kids who spilled cranberry juice on my art." She narrows her eyes at Renée. "Payback time. Take some of our Cat-astrophe flyers. You can pass them to your friends." She slaps a tall stack down on the counter.

"Someone else knocked into us," Renée reminds her.

"And then I bumped Star Loughead's hand. She's the one whose cranberry juice landed on your hanging."

Ms. Lacey turns to glare at me. "You put bags of dog scat in trees. Here's some extras for you." She piles more flyers on the stack and pushes them toward us.

"That wasn't us," Renée says. "It was Red, who owns the Pomeranian."

"At Noble Dog Walking, we pick up after other dog owners: 'It's the responsible thing to do.'" I quote Dad at the end. He also says it's good for business, keeping parks and paths clean of dog doo. Otherwise people will complain and no one will be able to walk animals anywhere. I take the flyers to be polite.

"So," Ms. Lacey says, "you're in to buy licences for these two?" She points at the dogs. Pong leaps hopefully for an imagined treat between her fingers.

"No. We're here because we want to borrow a snake trap," Renée answers.

Ms. Lacey grins. "A what?"

"You know, something where you lure snakes in with food and —"

She cuts me off. "We don't have anything like that."

"What about your squirrel trap?" Renée asks. "That worked really well for us last fall when one came down our chimney."

"Well, yes, but that was for squirrels," she answers.

Captain Obvious. "Can't we use it for a snake?" I ask.

"It wouldn't work. For one, the trap door shutting might cut the snake in two as it enters."

Mistake number seven clearly goes to Renée whose bright idea it was for us to walk for an extra hour to the Burlington Animal Shelter because for sure they would have a snake trap.

But then she makes it worse by giving Janet Lacey attitude.

"Okay. Maybe you don't have a snake trap. But isn't it your job to catch animals that escape from owners? Especially dangerous snaky-type animals?"

DAY ONE, MISTAKE EIGHT

When Janet Lacey folds her arms across her chest, I swear I can see the muscles ripple right through her shirt. She could probably win an arm wrestle with Attila. She leans heavily on the counter, looking Renée straight in the eye, lifting a heavy eyebrow. "Do you know the location of an exotic snake? If so, we will certainly catch it for you."

"No, that's the problem." Renée throws up her hands in frustration. "We don't know where he is!"

I take a breath and use my calmest voice. "It's probably loose somewhere in the owner's house."

Ms. Lacey nods. "Well, then, you definitely need a trap."

Renée turns around and makes a silent scream face that only I can see.

My calm voice goes one pitch higher. "But if you don't have one, who does?"

"Just make one. Here, let me show you. I think we have a pop bottle in the back." She gets up and goes into the back office. We hear some rattling and the dogs get restless. Cages of moving, smelly furry things line all the walls, after all. Ping pulls me to the ferret cage and stands on his hinds, whimpering and wagging at the little creature.

Then Ms. Lacey returns with an oversized plastic bottle. "We used to trap snakes all the time as kids."

I yank Ping back over to the counter. "Sit!"

He drops his haunches.

"So you want to cut this top part off, just below the neck of the bottle, right where it's wide. Like so." Ms. Lacey takes a large knife and digs the crooked edges of the blade into the plastic. Slowly, she saws through the plastic.

"Careful!" I can't help myself.

Ms. Lacey stops a moment to smile at me. "I'm a pro," she says, then continues.

Renée watches her hands closely. "Nice ring," she says.

"Thanks."

"Did you just get engaged?" There's Renée with those questions again. The ring does look extra sparkly and new on her finger.

"I did …" Ms. Lacey keeps sawing.

But what amazes me is that adults always answer Renée and feed her even more information. It's as though because she's smart, they feel they want to help her understand the world better.

"… to myself." Ms. Lacey grins up at us. "Thought I would buy a nice ring to celebrate."

"Why?" Renée asks.

"Got tired of waiting for the right guy. You know?" The bottle finally separates into two pieces and she drops the knife on the counter. "So I'm going to buy a house. Maybe have a baby. All by myself. Because I can." She makes two fists and bends her arms at the elbow, as if to show off her muscles. "Huuah!" she grunts.

Then she picks up the top piece of the bottle and sits it upside down on the bottom piece so that the neck becomes the end of a funnel. "See how?" She lifts the top again. "Pile some earth on the bottom. Then put your live mouse or rat inside. Top back on, like so. Duct-tape the edges to keep it on nice and snug."

"Live mouse?" Renée repeats, wincing.

"Are you actually going to throw yourself a wedding?" I blurt. I can't believe I asked that.

Ms. Lacey looks at me. "Of course. The presents will help with the house." Then she turns to Renée. "Yes, a live mouse. The snake comes in, swallows it, and gets too fat to fit back through the opening."

Renée grips the counter. Her voice squeaks a little. "But why can't it be a dead mouse?" she asks.

"Are you going to wear a white dress and everything?" Clearly, I've spent too much time with Renée.

Ms. Lacey grins again. "The works. I deserve the best." She spreads her fingers as if to admire her own ring.

"We have plenty of dead mice." Renée leans forward on her hands. A cat ready to pounce. "Why can't we use those?"

"They like their prey fresh. And movement attracts the snake. Punch a lot of little holes around the bottle, too, so the smell gets out."

"And the mouse can breathe!" Renée insists.

"Yeah, and that, too." She passes me the large bottle.

"Thanks. So I guess we need to trap a mouse first," I grumble. "Can we use the squirrel trap for that?"

Ms. Lacey cups a hand to her ear: "Did I hear someone say they want to adopt Mickey?" Then she winks. "Do you promise to give him a good home?" she asks us. "Here, give me that." She takes back the bottle and stabs it a few times. "Come with me."

Together we walk over to a little cage up against the other wall.

This one gets Pong's interest. He sits down tall in front of it. Ping yaps with excitement.

"Careful, don't let the dogs near there." Ms. Lacey points to a big white splotch on the wall. "Just repaired the drywall. Had a little trouble with the sheep last week."

"Sheep?" Renée and I repeat at the same time.

"Someone found him wandering. You'd think those things were docile. Man, you'd be wrong."

Nobody's anywhere near the drywall, anyway. The dogs behave pretty well considering all the interesting smells and sounds surrounding us.

Pong lifts his ears and tilts his head as Ms. Lacey dabs her thumb into a jar of peanut butter on the shelf below. Then she reaches into the cage. After a moment, a small brown mouse shakes himself loose of the cedar chips and crawls up Ms. Lacey's fingers. "He's been here since before me." She scoops him up, dumps him in the bottle, and puts the top back on. "Old timer. And they only live two or three years, max." We return to the front counter where Ms. Lacey places the bottle in full view. She tapes the lid on and heads for the back.

Mickey stands up with his small pink hands planted against the plastic wall. His nose twitches like crazy and his glossy eyes ask questions. His satellite ears seem to listen to us for answers.

"Awww. He's so cute," Renée says.

Ms. Lacey returns with a zip-lock bag of tiny pellets. "Mouse chow." She plunks it down beside the bottle.

Mickey eyeballs the bag, nose still twitching.

Ms. Lacey drops a few pellets down the hole and Mickey grabs one right away. "He's an active little guy. Your python should find him irresistible."

"Is there any way we can get him back out?"
Renée asks. "I mean, once the snake swallows him,
can we make it cough Mickey back up?"

"Nah. You'd have to slice the snake open. And
that would just be cruel."

Renée turns quiet. This is a mistake, I know it.
She's already too attached to Mickey. We're never
going to catch King this way.

"That will be ten dollars," Ms. Lacey says.

Mistake eight, I sigh. Reaching into my pants
pocket, I fish for some coin. "I only have five."
Maybe I can still stop this from happening.

"Good enough." Ms. Lacey scoops the change.
"Sign here." She passes me a form.

I borrow her pen.

"Usually, we ask your parents to sign since you're
underage. But I'll sign for you." I watch her diamond
flash as she scrawls something. She smiles up at me.

She's going to marry herself, *wow*. "Thanks." In a
kind of a trance, I take the bottle and walk to the door,
Pong close at my heels, Ping barking behind me.

"Wait!"

We turn back.

"You forgot your flyers!" She holds out the stack.
"Our cats need homes. After this week, we have to
make some hard decisions."

"You don't mean you'll put them down, do
you?" I ask.

Her smile droops. "We have to find homes!" she repeats, and waves the flyers.

Renée dashes to the counter and grabs them. We stuff them all in our pockets.

"Our felines thank you." Ms. Lacey waves and calls. "Bye Mickey. I'll miss you."

What kind of person marries herself?

DAY ONE, MISTAKE NINE

On the way back, Renée passes me the bottle with Mickey in it. "Here, you carry him."

Makes sense since I walk the easier, quieter dog. Tucked under my arm, the mouse won't get bumped around. For once, Renée doesn't have much to say.

Trying to get her out of her mood, I chuckle. "Imagine buying yourself an engagement ring."

"Nobody else will ever buy her one." She doesn't look at me, just keeps marching. "That woman has no heart."

"She likes cats."

"She doesn't like cats. If people don't adopt them on Monday, she's going to put them all down!"

"She didn't exactly say that. Anyhow, she likes snakes."

"Like Medusa. Snakes grow on her head."

"Good one." But Renée still isn't smiling, and even Ping has trouble keeping up with her.

"That's it." Renée punches her hand in the air. "We have to get people to adopt every last one of those cats."

"For sure. We'll give out those flyers. Talk it up."

Ping's tongue hangs out. Pong's panting hard.

"Why don't we go down by the creek and sit for a while?" I suggest. "The dogs look exhausted."

She sighs. "Fine."

"Fine," is not "Sure!" or "Great!" but the dogs and I do need a rest and there's a small park area around the creek, which will be perfect.

The red and gold leaves of the trees along the sidewalk hide the little gully. But I know where to find the set of stairs that leads down to the creek. I hesitate to take Pong down. The metal grating on each step looks sharp and pokey. "Not sure what that's like on paw pads," I tell Renée. "Let's just go down the hill."

I begin to slide, and Pong pulls me. Finally, I end up on my butt, keeping Mickey's bottle close to my chest till I reach the bottom.

A cement pipe, large enough for a Smart car to pass through, carries the water underneath the street, then over a brick ledge and down into the creek, mini-waterfall style. The water bubbles and gurgles around some rocks, a few of which have words written on them. I'm tired and just slump down on a large flat rock, placing Mickey in his bottle beside me. I loosen my grip on Pong's leash, and he sniffs among the bushes surrounding the water.

Ping, as usual, acts crazy, leading Renée around the stones, snuffling into the brush till he finds the perfect spot and begins to dig, throwing dirt up behind him.

"Hey, Attila," Renée suddenly calls. "What are you doing over there!"

Her brother struts out of the cement pipe, dipping his head to clear it. His mohawk stands about a foot up, though, so it brushes the ceiling. He's wearing a long-sleeved black T-shirt, which he's pushed up, and it's not all that warm. His arm muscles strain against the sleeves. In his hand, he grips a spray-paint can. "What does it look like I'm doing?"

I stand up again, and Pong and I stroll over to have a look. Inside the pipe is a painting of a three-headed serpent, each head with a red tongue flicking out. The body is a vibrant green with spots that are a sunset gold. My mouth drops open. "That's amazing. So lifelike."

"It's a mythical creature," Renée grumbles. "There aren't any live ones."

"Yes, that's true. But each head looks real …" His serpent actually looks like a ball python, ten times as big, maybe, with triple the number of heads, but otherwise, exactly the same spots and colours. "Say, Attila, do you use real models for your work?"

"Nah! Sometimes something real inspires me. You know, something catches my eye. I may use a photo. But no models."

"Why do you always have to do this?" Renée demands, throwing her arms up toward the pipe. "You're going to get in trouble again. Mom and Dad will fight …"

Attila frowns. "I can't resist the large surface." He throws his arms up, too, almost in the same way as Renée. Family thing, I guess. "I have things inside me that are too big for a little square or rectangle. They must come out on something as big as the idea itself."

"But it's against the law!" she says.

"Nobody will even see. Look at those rocks. People write messages on them all the time. That's graffiti, too."

Pong and I stroll closer to them. Flat and softball-sized, they aren't as big a canvas as Attila's pipes and bridges. *I need a job,* the message on one reads. Not that artistic. On another, two rocks over, it reads, *Harry loves Salma.* Those words have a heart around them. Another reads, *Blue Jays Rule,* even though they didn't even make the series this year. Another one stops me, it's so sad: *I can't marry you.*

Renée points out another one with her foot. "Hey, this one sounds good!"

10:15, Saturday, Oct 20. Freedom!

"Wow, precise," I say.

"We were in the park walking around, then," Renée answers, sounding more like herself again. "Saturdays always mean freedom. Even to adults."

"Here, why don't you guys try?" Attila holds out two black markers.

I grab one. Renée resists for a few moments, but he pushes it at her. "You must have something you want to get out from inside you."

I kneel down and the dogs gather around to lick my face. I pat them, scrub at their heads, loving the way they nudge me for more. Renée stares at Mickey.

Finally, I duck away from the dogs for a moment, find a potato-sized rock, and write in bold black letters, *Noble Dog Walking forever!*

I remember a time when there was no Noble Dog Walking service and Dad and Mom worked around the clock away from home, Dad in air traffic control. I hated it; I was scared all the time. I don't ever want to go back to that. But writing it in bold black letters makes me feel as though I've put a powerful wish out into the universe. I can see how painting big, huge things on bridges and water towers is a rush for Attila.

Renée frowns, chooses a slightly bigger stone, and then writes: *I want to keep Mickey.*

"Who's Mickey?" Attila asks.

"This mouse," she answers.

Attila crouches down for a moment, pushing Ping and Pong away so he can have a clear view of the pop bottle. "Well, I'm glad you got that out of your system, Renée. 'Cause Dad will never let you keep a rodent."

"Besides which," I add, "we need Mickey to catch our missing snake."

"Really? Stephen Noble, if you think you're going to take this cute little mouse to feed some big ugly snake, then you are sadly mistaken."

So number nine is a sad mistake.

"All we need is movement and smell to lure King into our trap, right?"

I nod.

"Well, then, we can use one of those frozen mice as a lure. We just need to be a little creative."

DAY ONE, MISTAKE TEN

We return Attila's markers and set off again for the Bennetts by a slightly different route. Good for developing the dogs' intelligence, and there are lots of Halloween decorations the way we're walking this time. Huge shaggy spiders hang from cotton spiderwebs on hedges and trees. Skeletons dance from porch lights. A few witches seem to have flown into garage doors and flattened themselves.

Pong strains to reach a haystack with a pumpkin-head scarecrow sitting on it. I step forward to grab him before he sprays it, and a voice groans, "Get off my grave!"

I jump.

Renée giggles and snorts.

I notice a waxy pair of hands reaching from the grass and edge back.

"If you think that's good, you should see Reuven's Frankenstein. When you walk up his path, he sticks out his arms and moans."

"His dad collects bottles on recycling day. Didn't think his family could afford high-tech decorations."

"They found the monster in the trash. Reuven fixed it up," Renée answers.

"Whoa, he's such a genius making stuff. Wonder if he'd partner with us next science fair," I say. He left his last project in his backpack in the computer lab. Because a bomb threat was sent to the school, a police robot came, mistook it for that bomb, and blew it up.

We cross the street to the Bennetts' house and the dogs slow down, knowing what's coming. I unlock the door, open it, and Renée has to drag Ping in. "C'mon, you've had a two-hour walk!"

I fill their water bowls, dole out kibble, and when they settle in their beds, give them each a liver bite and a pat. Meanwhile, Renée's on the cell phone.

"Reuven, we have a life and death situation and we need your help." Renée likes adding drama to everyone's life. "Uh-huh, uh-huh. What we need is for you to help us rig up a mouse corpse so that it moves and looks alive. No, not a Halloween decoration. Snake bait." She pauses.

"Uh-huh, uh-huh. And listen, would you have an old cage somewhere? For guinea pigs would be fine. A little bent is okay. Yeah, yeah. An exercise wheel might be nice. Yup. For sure, we owe you one." She waves a hand at me while she continues to talk. "Meet us at the corner of Overton and Cavendish. Five o'clock is good. At the house with the dumpster in the driveway."

It's twilight as Reuven makes the turn onto the walkway with his wagon full of junk. He's a short, wiry shadow outlined in gold by the sun's last rays. The contents of the wagon slide and he has to grab for them. Renée dashes back to help. Once they're closer, I see a cage, a pile of newspapers, a toolbox, and a small black box. "What is that thing anyway, Reuven? It looks like a bomb."

"You'll see." Close to the front door, I set the pop bottle with Mickey onto the ground. Then I look both ways before grabbing the key from under the flowerpot. We aren't doing anything wrong but it feels funny letting another kid into someone else's house.

Renée picks up Mickey's bottle and we lead Reuven, wagon and all, through the living room.

"No snake's been through here," he says. "You would see the slither marks in the drywall dust."

I shiver.

We roll through the kitchen and into the family room at the back of the house.

Reuven unloads the cage and hands Renée copies of the *Post*. "You can shred this for the cage, till you buy wood chips."

Renée immediately begins tearing up the paper and pitching it in the cage. I help her, and as we shred, Reuven picks up the defrosted mouse from the aquarium and carefully attaches wires to each of the mouse's four legs. "Your live mouse would probably like a toilet paper roll or a little box to hide in," he tells us.

"What are you, the mouse whisperer?" I ask.

He just grins.

Renée releases Mickey from the pop bottle into the cage. The live mouse sits there, wide-eared and mesmerized, watching as Reuven holds up the dead one. "Can you hold this for a second?" He passes it to me.

I grab the stiff body and he connects the main wire to the small bomb-like box. He plugs the bomb into an outlet.

"Just hold it by that wire, Stephen. Ready?"

Renée nods. I hunch my shoulders and wince.

Reuven flips the switch, and the dead mouse does a crazy-wild breakdance.

Okay, the small bomb is actually a motor. My mistake. Tiny one. Not even counting it.

"Can you maybe make him move a little slower?" Renée asks. "We don't want him to scare the snake away."

Reuven nods. "Sure." He fiddles with a knob on the motor. The mouse does a slow half cartwheel and then jerks back and repeats.

Creepy.

At the side of his cage closest to where the dead mouse spins, Mickey stands, two pink hands in the air. He looks like he's in love.

"Judging by Mickey's reaction, I'd say our lure is working," Renée says.

"Good. Put him in the pop bottle," I tell Reuven.

"Okay." He turns off the motor and places the mouse in the bottom of the bottle, with the main wire hanging out through the opening. "Flip the switch, Renée."

She does, and the corpse becomes a mouse mar-
ionette. Renée gives him a thumbs-up. "Perfect,
Reuven. With all Mickey's mouse poop in the bottle, we should have great mouse smell, too."

Reuven smiles as he stares at his handiwork.
"Are you sure the snake is small enough to fit
through the opening?"

Renée's eyebrows lift.

"Sure, a ball python's tiny," I bluff. "If the hole
were any bigger, the snake would fit through even
after the mouse was in his gut."

"Okay. Well, you better keep checking so that the
python doesn't digest the mouse and escape. Now,
remember how you said you'd owe me one …?"

This is where our big mistake of the day comes in.

"Sure. Anything, anytime," Renée says without
negotiating terms.

Reuven grins. "Tomorrow is a special flyer day
for my paper delivery. I would like you to show up
at ten thirty so you can help me insert the flyers and
then deliver the newspapers with me."

Could be number ten — accidentally agreeing to
help deliver Reuven's newspapers on the day when
they are heaviest.

"Okay," Renée says. "We have a special flyer of
our own." She hands him a Cat-astrophe poster.
"Have you ever thought of adopting a cat?"

"No. My parents don't like extra mouths to

feed." He looks it over, anyway. "They're on sale? My family does like a bargain. Maybe my cousins would buy one."

"Spread the word," Renée says.

We clear out of the house, Mickey's cage on Reuven's wagon. In the light of the fuzzy grey moon, the cars on the street seem streaked with chalk. At least, I *assume* it has to be a trick of the moonlight.

We're right next door to my house when Renée notices.

"What is this white stuff on Mr. Lebel's Mustang?" She leans closer to the passenger door.

"Don't touch!"

Too late. Renée rubs her finger on the streak along the door panel. This beats the newspaper-flyer thing. Touching the Mustang is the huge mistake of the day. It wins the number-ten spot. The car alarm blares.

DAY ONE, MISTAKE ELEVEN

Everyone ignores car alarms except for Mr. Lebel, apparently. He runs out of the house in his boxers and undershirt, shaking his fists in the air. "Get away from my car!"

He doesn't shut his alarm off.

Honk, honk, honk.

"Sorry, I was just trying to get the white stuff off." Renée's brow knits. *Honk, honk, honk.* "But it's not coming off."

"You kids!" he shouts. *Honk, honk, honk.* He moves closer. He's hairy, and not just his chest. Finally, he thumbs his key to shut the alarm. As he bends down and squints at the streak, we can see tufts of brown fur peeking out from the arm and neck holes of his undershirt. "You spray-painted my Mustang?" It was a howl of pain. Maybe a werewolf howl.

"No, sir. We most certainly did not," Reuven said. "We were just bringing home Renée's new pet when we happened to notice."

"Check out our wagon. We don't have any paint with us," I said.

"Anyhow, this paint is already dry," Renée added.

"It's dried on?" Mr. Lebel howls again. He licks his finger and tries to rub at the white streak. The paint doesn't come off, not even a little.

Renée whips out a Cat-astrophe brochure. "Maybe this is the wrong time to suggest this but … would you be interested in owning a cat?"

Mr. Lebel growls. Werewolves are clearly not cat fans.

Beethoven's Fifth suddenly plays from Renée's pocket. Saved by the music. She takes out her cell and checks a text. As she reads, her mouth buckles and she shakes her head like she can't believe the message.

"What's wrong, Renée?" I ask softly.

She takes a breath and straightens. "Mr. Lebel, you should call the police. It seems they've already arrested someone for vandalizing several cars in the neighbourhood."

"Really? I will." And without an apology, good-bye, or Cat-astrophe flyer, he runs back into the house.

"You shouldn't touch other people's cars," Reuven says.

"Leave it!" I warn him, something I say to Pong when he wants to eat a dead squirrel. We walk to the next house, my house. Renée's still not talking. I don't even want to ask. "Have they arrested Attila again?"

She nods. "But you know how much he loves cars. And yeah, he loves spray-painting large surfaces. But he creates art, not skunk streaks!"

"Why would they arrest your brother?" Reuven asks.

"Because when the police went out to investigate, they caught him coming home from his serpent creation."

"And he was carrying his paint!" I say.

I'm about to turn off to my house.

Renée stops, too. I know what she has in mind. I don't blame her. She turns to Reuven. "Well, thanks a lot for helping us with our dead mouse–mobile." Renée lifts Mickey's cage out of his wagon.

"You're welcome. I can take your live mouse all the way to your house if you like."

And here it comes.

"No. That's okay. I'm hoping Mr. Noble will let me sleep over. There'll be a lot of arguing going on at my house tonight."

"All right. See you tomorrow at ten thirty," Reuven says.

I groan. Flyer and newspaper delivery.

"Bye," Renée says. "Don't forget about the cat sale."

We walk around Dad's car to get to our front door. The Grape-mobile is purple with the Noble Dog Walking paw print logo on the side. "At least *our* car hasn't been painted."

"People may be suspicious if it's the only one that didn't get sprayed."

"True." I frown and sigh. Another crime to solve. Not just to clear Attila's name, but also Noble Dog Walking's. After all, I want Dad's business to last forever. That's what I wrote on the rock.

But I can't even think how to prove anyone's innocence just now. So I switch problems. "What are you going to do about Mickey? Put him in the shed?"

"C'mon, Stephen. It's too cold. And what if there's a cat out there? We absolutely know a ball python is on the loose."

"You think you're taking a rodent into our house? With my mom so allergic to dander?"

"*All* animal dander? Has she even been tested for mice? How much dander can the tiny guy have?"

"Look. I know Dad will let *you* stay, but Mickey ..."

"How about I head straight to the bathroom upstairs. You distract him."

"Okay." I open the door slowly, head ducking around it to see if the coast is clear. "Dad?"

"Hi, Stephen," his voice calls from the living room. "Hey, Renée! What's in the cage?"

"What's plan B?" I ask her.

She makes her silent scream face, hangs up her jacket with one hand, and goes into the living room with Mickey.

I hang up mine, too, and follow.

Dad's sitting back on his easy chair, feet up, his hair mussed. He's knitting — something he likes to do when he needs to relax — only he's doing it at a breakneck speed. The needles in his hand make a little *click-click* sound. A small red sweater grows from the bottom. Rose's sweater.

"Hey, Mr. Noble. How are you?" She sits down on the couch with the cage on her lap. Mickey's curled up under a pile of newspaper shreds.

"Not great." The needles click-click furiously. "I was called in to the police station for questioning. Mason Man's missing a phone and a laptop. He's accused me."

"You got my text, right, Dad?

"No, I did not. Didn't charge my phone because of the power outage."

"Sorry, Dad. He called you when you were out. Asked for his key back."

"Yeah, well, he's got that now. Saw your brother at the station, Renée." He puts his knitting down and looks up at her. "You're going to have to go home sometime."

He knows the routine by now. Every time Attila's in trouble with the law, Renée wants a sleepover. Even if it's in the middle of the week.

"It's like I'm not even there, Mr. Noble. All they do is yell about Attila."

"It's rough. I'm sorry. You're welcome to stay tonight." He smiles at her, waits a moment to change the subject, and then looks down at the cage. "Oooh, what a cute little guy. What's his name?"

"Mickey." Renée launches into the story about Noble's missing new client, King.

Gah, I wish she'd let me tell him.

"Stephen, you should have mentioned this earlier," Dad says as he picks up his knitting again. His eyes twitch.

"You were already so worried about Mrs. Irwin." Instead I tell him about the trip to the animal shelter for the trap — *clicketty-click-click*, his knitting speeds up — about the clerk who wants to marry herself. *Click, click, click, click!* We give him one of the Cat-astrophe flyers. "Fifty percent off all cats. And free neutering, too!"

"Some of my clients might want a cat." He puts down the knitting, takes one, and looks at it for a moment. "My one client, heh-heh. We could expand. Do some cat sitting."

We talk about the live mouse versus dead mouse bait thing.

"But then, Reuven made a dead mouse into this amazing animated thing! So we get to keep Mickey." Renée reaches into the cage for Mickey. "Isn't that great?"

Dad watches Mickey scramble up Renée's arm. "He's hand-trained. They must have treated him well at the animal shelter."

Renée raises one eyebrow. "Hardly. She was willing to let him go as snake bait. Do you think we can teach him to do tricks?"

"Absolutely. Stephen, get a paper towel tube from the recycling. And my jar of cashews."

His special jar of cashews? He's giving those nuts to the mouse? I have to shuffle things around in the cupboard to find the jar. I grab the tube from the bin, and by the time I come back from the kitchen, Dad and Renée are kneeling on the floor, heads together. Something twists inside me.

He likes Renée. Daughter he never had and all that. But I've only had Dad at home for a few months and Mom's hardly ever around. It's hard for me to share him. For just one moment, I want to hurl cashews at them, one at a time, like a jealous squirrel.

But that would be a mistake.

I feel sorry for Renée, her father and her brother being such grumps, after all.

So I just kneel down on the other side of Dad, place the tube on the floor, and open the jar. Renée takes a nut, and Dad lowers the hand with Mickey in it. Mickey twitches his nose as he investigates the tube opening, and Renée holds the nut at the other end of the tube.

Mickey dashes through, lands next to Renée's hand, and sits up tall. Then he grabs the cashew in his own long pink fingers and nibbles.

"Good boy!" I tell the mouse. Renée lets me have a turn holding him and I pat his tiny head with my finger.

"All right. Put Mickey back in his cage and wash your hands before supper," Dad tells us. "Use soap," he adds.

Upstairs in the bathroom, Renée and I scrub up with plenty of Mom's green-tea hand soap. Even after rinsing and drying, my hands smell so good they make me feel hungry for fortune cookies. Back in the kitchen, we set the table as Dad's special spaghetti sauce bubbles up on the stove. The aroma of tomato and oregano pops into the air. Mmmm.

Dad makes the thin angel hair pasta I love. Turns out Renée likes it, too. I wash the lettuce and Renée cuts up some cucumber and celery. Salad, spaghetti, and sauce topped with some cheese: team work, and it's all delicious.

Later we watch some YouTubes on how to train your mouse. They aren't dogs, you can't cuddle them or anything, but they are smart. One video showed mice walking backward, kind of like that moonwalking dance move.

When we finally go to bed, it's late and Mickey bunks in the guest room with Renée.

I know I'll fall asleep the second my head hits the pillow. It's been a long day. No more mistakes for any of us.

My eyes grow heavy, heavier, and then … suddenly, I bolt upright. My digital clock flashes the time as 11:58. This has to be my final mistake for the day. The bonus number eleven. I jump out of my bed, dash over to the guest bedroom door, and rap on it. "Renée, we forgot. We have to check on our snake trap!"

day two

THE GREAT MISTAKE

MYSTERIES

Renée agrees that it has to be right now — it can't wait for morning. Best of all, she doesn't suggest I just go by myself. She's already dressed in my old sweatpants and T-shirt, so she waits as I throw track pants and a sweater over my pajamas. At 12:01 we pass Dad's bedroom and hear his snoring right through the door. It's a strange, loud, rumbly inhale, followed by a puff, puff, puff exhale. *Roghhhhhh! Pewt, pewt, pewt, pew.* We tiptoe down the stairs.

I pass Renée her jacket. Flyers fall out of a pocket and she scoops them up and stuffs them back in. I grab my own coat and we make our break, out the door and across the street.

Street lights are on. It's a perfect Saturday night, no wind, warm for October. A couple of skateboards rattle down the middle of the street. Our principal's son, Serge, rides one; Red, the guy with the Pomeranian, rides the other. It's the second time we've seen them together.

Wonder why Red would hang out with him? You'd think Serge would be a model student with a principal as a parent, but I'm pretty sure he's only out on parole.

More houses have been decorated for Halloween today. A couple actually have twinkling orange and black lights. There's a pile of orange plastic pumpkins on the next porch and a white sheet ghost hangs from the tree in the yard.

Around the corner I spot the Diamond Drywall van hurtling our way, and I try not to worry that it's going to run the skateboarders down.

"Do you think there's a drywall emergency somewhere?" Renée asks as it approaches.

"No." I squint and see two passengers in the front. "Just the drywall guy using the van for a date."

The decorations at the next house really creep me out. A strip of yellow caution tape fences off the scene of a massacre. Plastic limbs with red stumps are scattered near black crosses. A pale, severed Styrofoam head sits on a stump; a cardboard, double-bladed battle-axe lies on the ground next to it.

"Boo!" Star jumps out from behind the hedge. The bright street light turns her face ghostly white.

"Aaaah!" My heart leaps into my mouth.

"What are you doing out at this hour?" Renée asks her.

"Why? It's not past my bedtime yet." All in black — leggings, long-sleeved sweater, and knitted cap — Star looks like a ninja, except for the star-shaped sparkle in her nose. "You guys, on the other hand, should be in bed."

"We're checking on our snake trap," I answer.

"Cool. I'm on the hunt for a missing spray-paint can. White. Attila thought he'd left it near the creek but I looked everywhere."

"Does he usually leave his paint cans near his graffiti?" I ask.

"Sometimes. Till he's finished. The spot wasn't exactly high traffic." She shrugs her shoulders. "But it's missing. And I bet only the kid who sprayed all the cars knows where it is."

"You're trying to prove Attila's innocence," Renée says.

"That's right. The police want to make him for the two break-ins, too. He's a bodybuilder — so what? Doesn't mean he wants to steal a Mr. Universe medal."

"He has his own phone," Renée adds. "Probably a more up-to-date one than Mr. Mason has. And a pretty great computer. Grandma bought it for when he goes to college."

Attila still has about another eight months of high school, so he seems pretty spoiled with technology. Still, I don't think people steal electronics for their own personal use. But pointing that out to Renée doesn't seem like a good idea.

"I wonder which car was the last one to be

vandalized," Star says. "He probably ran out of paint then and trashed the can nearby."

"Mr. Lebel's Mustang. Next door to us," I answer. "Because he didn't spray our car."

"Okay. I'll check near your house. In the meantime, if you really want to catch snakes, you should head down to the creek."

"We're looking for a particular snake," Renée says. "Before you go, can we interest you in the animal shelter's Cat-astrophe blowout cat sale?" She pulls a flyer from her jacket pocket and pushes it at Star.

"Maybe." Star looks at the brochure as she saunters off.

At King's house, we turn up the walkway and I grab the key from under the flowerpot. Click, the door creaks open. The house is dark.

"Are snakes nocturnal?" I whisper to Renée.

"They come out whenever they want to, Stephen." She flips on a light switch. "As long as it's warm enough."

With all the windows shut, it feels toasty. Still no slither marks in the drywall dust on the living room floor. We make our way carefully to the family room at the back, switching on more lights as we go. I can hear the whirring noise before I get there. "Drat. Zombie mouse is still doing his thing."

"What do you think? Should we leave him on?" Renée asks.

I shake my head. "I don't think there's any point. King can't be here. And with our luck, we'll start an electrical fire."

"Let's put a new mouse in the aquarium, just in case he's still here somewhere." She goes to the freezer and, wrinkling her nose, takes out a frozen body. "Should we nuke him?"

"No! Just take the wrapper off."

Meanwhile, I unplug our zombie mouse, throw him in one of my dog-doo bags, and pack up the little motor to return to Reuven. Renée turns off all the lights. We back out of the house, and I slip the key back under the winter cabbage.

"Here now!" a cannon-shot voice calls out.

I look up and see Mr. Rupert clomping our way in big black boots and a camouflage military uniform. Jumping to a wrong conclusion, he grabs my shoulder. The first mistake-of-the-day award goes to him.

"What are you kids stealing from that house?"

DAY TWO, MISTAKE TWO

I try to shrug him off but his grip is tight.

"Let Stephen go!" Renée squints hard at him.

He releases me but takes out his cell phone. "I'm calling the police!"

"Don't!" Renée grabs his arm this time.

I can't believe she did that. He is so scary.

Quickly, I explain. "We're not taking anything that doesn't belong to us." I lift up the bottle so he can see. "This is a snake trap!"

"And that other thing, what's that? Looks like a bomb."

"No," Renée answers. "It's a motor. Makes the mouse move so the snake thinks it's alive."

He doesn't ask about the little black bag with the dead mouse in it. "You say you were trying to catch a snake in a house? Why not the creek? Saw one there the other day."

"We're not trapping snakes for fun," I explain. "The owner's pet python got loose."

"Noble Dog Walking was hired to look after the python," Renée adds.

Mr. Rupert shakes off Renée's hand. "Tell it to the cops. There have been two break-ins this week. And car vandalism!" His thumb hovers over the phone screen. He taps once, twice.

Renée touches his arm, gently this time. "Mr. Rupert, have you ever thought of adopting a cat?"

"What?" he sputters but stops tapping.

"You know …" Her voice soothes now. "You walk the streets after midnight. You must be lonely."

"I patrol, not walk. Someone has to keep the neighbourhood safe."

"Do the police like that?" I ask. "Aren't you out

on probation? You're not carrying your replica gun, are you?"

While the street light made Star look pale, it turns Mr. Rupert's face a deep shade of tomato soup. "My taxes pay their salary!" he huffs, but his thumb closes the screen and he slides his cell phone back into his pocket.

"This Monday the animal shelter is having a sale. Half off, and you can get your cat neutered for free," Renée tells him.

He frowns. "My wife always wanted one."

"Here. Take a flyer." Renée yanks another one from her jacket pocket. "Think about it. Pets lower your blood pressure. And cats aren't that much work."

He looks confused. Renée has that effect on me sometimes, too. I keep explaining to him. "Mr. Rupert, *we're* trying to catch the criminals, too. My dad's business is at stake. We're losing customers."

"My brother Attila's been questioned," Renée adds.

"You shouldn't be out at night!" Mr. Rupert says.

"You shouldn't be 'patrolling,' either." Renée makes air quotes with her fingers.

"I ought to tell your parents," Mr. Rupert says.

"We should team up," I suggest instead.

"Share information!" Renée adds. "Did you see the Diamond Drywall van earlier?"

"Someone needs to report him. Speeding like that." He shakes his head.

"Unsafe," I agree. "Especially with the skate-boarders in the middle of the street."

"I hate house flippers anyway. Skateboarders, too, for that matter."

Kids, dogs, and people in general. "The drywall guy is a house flipper, too?" I ask.

"You must know." Mr. Rupert raises his eye-brows. "He's your snake owner!"

"We were hired by a woman," I quickly explain. "She's away. Left on a plane." Does over-explaining make me sound guilty?

"They're a couple," Mr. Rupert says. "The dry-wall guy and her."

"Mr. Rupert, that's great information," Renée exclaims. "But we should head home now. I think I saw a flashing red light. Police may be heading this way."

Mr. Rupert marches off quickly.

"Do you think we can trust him?" I ask her as we walk in the other direction toward home.

"No. I don't think we should trust Star, either. Both of them are suspects. But you know what they say, keep your friends close ..."

"And your enemies closer," I finish.

When we get home, I slip the dead mouse into the trash in the garage. Then we sneak back into the house and head up the stairs to the music of Dad's strange snore. *Roghhhhhh! Pewt, pewt, pewt, pew.*

So deep asleep, he'll never know about us leaving the house after midnight. And tomorrow being Sunday, we can sleep in, anyway. "Good night," I tell Renée.

"Sleep tight," she answers.

I strip down to my pajamas and bury myself in blankets for a great, long snooze. I close my eyes.

But my mind tries to sort through all the details that float through my thoughts: a missing snake, an empty ring box, spray-painted cars, a stolen phone and laptop, a stolen Mr. Universe medal. What do they have in common? Not Noble Dog Walking. Can't *just* be Noble Dog Walking.

My thoughts tumble and spin like clothes in a washing machine. Somehow, I end up in a strange scene. A wedding. I see Janet Lacey in a long, white gown, and she's walking toward the counter at the animal shelter.

On all sides, she's surrounded by cats. Hundreds of them: large and small, tiger-striped, and spotted orange and black. They're mewing and meowing, and she's walking to the beat of their sounds. So weird.

I know she's marrying herself, so what will happen when she reaches the counter?

The cats part, and I see a large gold coin hanging from the counter — we're talking dinner-plate-sized — with a blue and white ribbon attached to it. I can make out Mr. Sawyer's face on the polished mirror surface, so that's how I know it has to be his Mr. Universe medal. I also somehow know that Ms. Lacey is marrying it, which sounds crazy, but it's not any crazier than her marrying herself when you think about it.

From the cat gallery, a cell phone plays a tune — the theme from one of Dad's favourite dog shows, *The Littlest Hobo*. Cats turn and hiss at the cell phone owner who, of course, is Dad. He shrugs but answers it, nodding his head. Then he holds it out toward me and calls, "Stephen, it's for you. Mom's calling."

And that's when I wake up. But I can still hear Dad. "Phone! Stephen! Are you up yet?"

Blam, blam, blam, he pounds on my door. "Stephen! Mom's on the line."

I open my eyes. I'm not dreaming anymore. I sit up. "Come in, Dad."

The door opens and he hands me the phone.

"Hi, Stephen."

"Mom." I blink and yawn. "How are you?"

"So good, now that I'm talking to you."

I can hear her smile as she talks and I struggle to shake off my sleepiness. Everything always seems better when she calls. "Mom, King's missing."

"Oh no, that's too bad. Poor Salma. She came onto the plane weeping about having to break up with her boyfriend."

"Were they engaged?" I ask, still thinking about my strange wedding dream.

"She wasn't wearing a ring. But I didn't ask. She was crying so much, everyone was looking at her."

"Did you say *she* broke up with him?" I ask. "Why was she crying?"

"Maybe she really didn't want to. But she said he never finished things he started, didn't clean up around the house."

I'll say, I thought, remembering all the drawers hanging open and the sheets on the floor.

"But she showed me a photo of him and he was hot! Some kind of bodybuilder. Does drywall, but I gather he doesn't work that much."

"A bodybuilder?" I repeat and think about that exercise room back at King's house.

"Yeah, lifts weights but won't lift a finger." Mom laughs and I laugh along, too.

"Anyway," Mom continues, "she was worried he wouldn't feed her pet snake. Revenge, you know. And she was going to be away three days. So I asked where she lived. Anything to stop her crying. Figured Dad could drive there and make sure. When she told me her address, I knew you could help her."

"Well, there was an awful storm here when you called yesterday morning, Mom."

"I know. Takeoff was delayed."

"We didn't get there till later. But there was a mouse in the aquarium."

"So King should have been fine. You wouldn't believe it. The man ahead of Salma somehow got it into his head that a snake had escaped on the plane and that's why we were delaying takeoff."

"That's just silly."

Mom doesn't say anything for a second.

"Right?" I say. "I mean, that's never happened before, has it? A snake loose in an airplane?"

"Well … once. On Air India. I heard they had to remove some seats to fit a stretcher in. And after they put the seats back in, some passengers noticed a snake curled up in one."

"What did you do?" I ask.

"Me? I never worked for Air India."

"No. For that guy who thought a snake was loose on your plane."

"Well, that was ridiculous. I think he'd had too much to drink. With the sheets of rain coming down and the lightning, there was no doubt about why we were delaying. We told him to calm down or get off the plane."

"That worked?"

"That and an extra bag of cashews."

Just like Mickey, I think. "We're hoping King will find his way back in the aquarium. We gave him a fresh mouse. When is King's owner getting back?"

"Monday evening."

"In time for the Cat-astrophe."

"What's that?"

"The animal shelter's having a cat sale, and the lady there gave me some flyers to pass around."

"That's nice …" I can hear voices in the background. "Listen, Stephen. I have to go. I hope Salma's snake comes back. But don't worry too much about it. I love you!" *Click!*

"I love you too, Mom." I stare at the receiver and miss her for another long moment. Then I take a breath and head downstairs for the kitchen, where Dad is making breakfast.

Before I can put the phone back in the cradle, it rings again and I see the name of the caller in the window. Mr. Rupert. Here's where I make mistake number two of the day. Before Mr. Rupert can snitch on us, I rush to confess about sneaking out of the house after midnight.

"Dad, you know how we set that snake trap up with the dancing dead mouse? We realized, late last night, that we needed to check on it. So we could make sure King didn't escape. Only, Mr. Rupert saw us. I think that's why he's calling now."

DAY TWO, MISTAKE THREE

"You mean you went out after we'd all gone to bed? How can I trust you anymore?" Dad shakes his head but finally picks up the phone like it's a smoking gun. "Hello? Yes. He's sitting right here. Sure." Dad hands me the receiver.

"Hi, Mr. Rupert."

"I found the paint can."

That's why he's calling? "Really? Where?"

"Pretty close to your friend Renée's house. Next door, actually. North side."

Reuven Jirad's house. But Reuven was with us the whole time.

"Right where her brother might have thrown it on his way home," Mr. Rupert continues.

"It's not Attila, Mr. Rupert. It can't be Attila." If only for Renée's sake. So much for the thief leaving the can behind where the trail of painted cars ended. "Do you think the police will want it as evidence?"

"Yes. I'll have to tell them where I found it. It won't look good for him."

And some of Attila's fingerprints are bound to be on it.

"Well, I've given you plenty of information," he continued. "Here's a question for you. Who else knows about the Mr. Universe medal? Besides Mr. Sawyer himself?"

"Anybody who went into Mrs. Irwin's studio, I guess."

"Right. Well, I'll leave that with you," he says and hangs up.

"Goodbye to you too!" I put the receiver down and face Dad.

"You are grounded."

Right on cue, Renée stumbles sleepily into the kitchen as if following the scent of pancakes.

"And Renée …"

Her head flips to attention at the mention of her name.

"You need to go home. Tell your parents about going out last night. You cannot come here and then head out at all hours of the night."

Renée's mouth drops open, then shuts again. "Can I have breakfast first?"

At this point, the phone rings a third time. Dad picks up. "Hello, Mrs. Kobai. Yes. Yes, well something's come up … I see. Oh. That's too bad. Sure." Dad's eyebrows huddle like storm clouds. "Do you want to speak to her? I understand. Perhaps that's best. All right. That's okay. Tomorrow's a day off for them, anyway. Don't give it another thought." He hangs up and frowns.

"Did something happen? Are my parents okay?" Renée asks.

"They're fine," Dad says so quietly that it's hard to believe they are. "But … they have things they need to work out. Your mom asked if you could stay here another night."

Renée's lip trembles.

It's one thing when you want to stay over at a friend's house; it's another when your parents don't even want you to come home.

Dad sets a plate on the table. "Sit, everybody. We have pancakes." His smile looks toothy fake and his eyes beg me to help. "Chocolate spread, too. If you like."

"Chocolate and syrup! Even better," I tell Renée. "Yay!" I try to sound cheery. I should be happy. Mrs. Kobai's call seems to have changed Dad's focus. Renée will sleep over again — so how is that in any way being grounded?

I push my luck a little harder. "Dad, we promised we would help Reuven with his paper route today. Also, can we walk Ping and Pong? After that, you can ground me forever, if you like."

"Grounding isn't supposed to be convenient," he snaps.

A tear slides down Renée's cheek.

Dad bites his lip. "We're going to wait till your mother gets home to discuss your punishment. So do the papers today, and walk the dogs."

"And we can give out cat flyers. Right, Renée? Maybe everyone will adopt a kitty and Janet Lacey won't have to …" I stop myself.

Another tear slides down her cheek.

"I'm just going to get my knitting." Dad escapes to the living room.

"C'mon, Renée." I pull out a kitchen chair for her. "We'll stop at Mrs. Irwin's house. Mr. Rupert wants to know who else knows about the Mr. Universe medal. That could be an important clue. And if we find the real criminal, your mom and dad will be happy again."

She makes a sad cough noise, and her shoulders shake.

Dad comes back in the room with the little yellow sweater he's knitting and the long striped scarf Renée's working on. "Here, maybe this will make you feel better."

He didn't bring me my knitting project but that's okay. I stab three pancakes and load them on my plate, cover them in chocolate, and drown them in syrup. Food calms me, knitting doesn't. Especially when Renée knits so much better. I pour myself a glass of milk and chow down to the rhythm of clicking needles.

"Hey, Dad. Did Buddy's owner get in touch with you?" I ask, trying to keep the air time from going all sad-quiet.

He looks up from his knitting.

"You know that Rotti named Buddy? His owner usually wears bright track suits?"

"No, she didn't call me. What did she want?"

"To hire you. Something about a new contract."

"Ahh, her cleaning business. Maybe that's what I

should get into next." Dad knits frantically. It's like he's under a spell.

Next? What about Ping and Pong? I take another big bite of pancake, but despite all the syrup and chocolate, the sweetness is gone.

"I'm out of green." Renée puts her scarf down. "I'll wait till you're done with yellow and add a stripe of that colour." She grabs a plate and takes a pancake. She's quieter than usual but at least she's not crying.

"If you finish in time, Dad, we can take Goldie's sweater over to Mrs. Irwin."

Renée cuts up her pancake and the knife screeches across the plate. "Thank you for the delicious breakfast," she says politely.

"You're welcome." *Click, click, click.* "Give me another half-hour and I'll be done. By the way, I did the laundry once the power came on. Your dog-walking uniforms are lying on the couch, clean and ready for you."

We finish eating and pick up our uniforms. I take a shower and put on the clean pants and shirt. Then I join Renée in the guest room. She's already dressed in the official Noble Dog Walking uniform. She sprawls on the floor, talking softly to Mickey, two fingers guiding his face. She holds a cashew in front of his nose while gently nudging him backward. She's doing it! She's training him to walk backward!

"Finished the sweater!" Dad yells from the living room.

Renée kisses the top of Mickey's head, puts him back in his cage, washes her hands, and then races me downstairs.

Dad holds up Goldie's new yellow sweater — small and bright with an orange and indigo trim.

"Nice work, Mr. Noble," Renée says and fingers the tiny, perfect stitches.

"I'll get a bag for it." He disappears for a minute and returns with a recycled birthday gift bag.

Renée takes the bag and places the little sweater in it. She also brings our stacks of Cat-astrophe flyers and the motor and wires from our snake trap to return to Reuven.

"Let's put it all in my backpack," I suggest. First I dump my books, agenda, and pencil case, and then we load in all the stuff.

"Careful with that sweater," Dad says and we put the little bag in last, on top of all the wires and flyers.

I hand Renée her jacket and then slip into my own. Despite the bright yellow sunshine and clear blue skies, the fall air feels just crisp enough for us to need jackets this morning as we head for the Bennetts' house.

When we reach their door, Ping jumps up and down in front of the picture window, barking happily. A jack-in-the-box. Pong stands tall and quiet beside him, front paws on the ledge, tail wagging.

That's when I discover a horrific mistake. I pat down all my pockets. Mistake number three will get us all fired for sure. "Renée, I've lost the Bennetts' key!"

DAY TWO. MISTAKE FOUR

"No, you didn't lose it, Stephen. This is a temporary misplacement. Can you remember where you had the key last?" Renée asks.

"In my pocket, this pocket!" I unbutton the top right pocket of my pants, reach deep inside, pull out the lining. Nothing.

"Check the others, just in case!"

I unbutton and pull out the linings on all four pockets, even the back ones. Nothing. I check my shirt pockets, although I hardly ever put anything there except maybe a pen. "What am I going to do? We have to feed them" — my voice breaks — "and walk them." I'm hyperventilating.

"It's okay. Calm down." She dumps the little dog sweater into the backpack and hands me the gift bag. "Breathe into this." Renée knits her brow. "Just a minute, Ping!" she calls to the little dog, still springing up and down.

When Pong barks once, I whimper. Pong rarely makes a sound.

"Take it easy." She pats my back. "I just had a thought. There are four spots most people hide a spare key."

"What are they?" I moan.

"Check the top of the doorframe."

I reach up and run my hand along it. "No key there."

That's one.

Renée lifts the doormat. No luck.

That's two.

"Under that flowerpot?" Renée suggests.

I lift it. Nothing.

That's three.

"Aha!" Renée runs to a strange-looking rock at the side of the walkway. "The old fake-stone trick." She lifts it.

That's four.

She pulls out a key. Grinning, she hands me it.

"Here's hoping." I stick it in the key slot and turn. *Click!* The door unlocks.

I exhale. "Thanks, Renée."

"No worries." She pushes open the door and Ping jumps on her leg. He runs his front paws up and down her knee frantically, and she coos and pats him.

Pong just leans his tall body against my thigh and I scrub around his ears.

"C'mon, let's get you guys some breakf—" Before I can finish the word, the dogs skitter across the floor to the kitchen.

Renée fills their water bowls, while I open a can of dog food. Ears at attention, the dogs train their eyes on me, watching my every move. Three-quarters of the can goes into Pong's dish, the last quarter into Ping's.

"Doesn't seem fair, eh, Ping? Just 'cause you're smaller," Renée says. "I know how it is."

I count for the dogs before setting the bowls down, training them to be patient. "One, two, three … and go!"

Ping wolfs down his food in seconds and tries to squeeze under Pong to get at his. Pong pushes his bowl away from him with his paw. He digs in. Ping moves closer. Still eating, Pong nudges the food bowl farther away with his nose. Ping sneaks in again. The bowl moves under snout power. Finally, Pong is done, too, and the dance ends.

For dessert, we move to the entrance, dogs following, and I hold out one of Dad's liver bites in each of my closed fists. I don't have to say a word; the dogs instantly drop down their butts to a beautiful tall sit in front of me. That's when I snap on their leashes and open my hands. They hoover up the little squares and then scramble to the door. I pass Ping's leash to Renée.

Out we go. Carefully, I lock the door behind us and put the key under the fake rock again. "I don't know what I'm going to say to Dad about losing the key."

"Nothing. We'll look everywhere in your room and find it!"

I shrug my shoulders. "Let's hope so. In the meantime, we better drop off Goldie's sweater to Mrs. Irwin so we can get to delivering newspapers."

"Right," Renée agrees, and we jog with the dogs.

It feels like we're getting better at running these days. "Hey, maybe we should try out for track," I suggest in between huffing and puffing.

Renée stops and hangs her head down to catch her breath. She gives me a sideways look, much like Ping does when he finds kibble in his bowl instead of canned dog food.

"Just kidding," I tell her. It's turned really warm outside by now, so I take off my jacket and tie it around my waist.

We stroll down the street a few blocks, dogs pulling, and I spot Mr. Ron crouched beside Mrs. Whittingham's shiny black van. She uses it to pick up and deliver her daycare kids.

Renée shakes her fist. "We've caught him white-handed!"

"Really? Let's take a closer look." I know she wants to find him spray-painting. Prove Attila innocent.

But Mr. Ron doesn't seem to care if the whole world watches, so he can't be doing anything illegal.

In fact, as we get closer, I hear him whistling cheerfully. He stops when we reach him, turns, and points at us. "Don't worry, be happy!" he says, then he continues whistling and rubbing at the van. Beside him on the pavement sits one of those large red gasoline jugs.

"Mr. Ron. What are you doing?" I ask.

"Isn't it obvious?" He straightens up and grins at us. "I'm cleaning off the paint from Mrs. Whittingham's van." He wags a finger. "Discovered a formula while cleaning the boss's truck. Yup, yup, yup. Cheaper than repainting." Mr. Ron steps back to admire his work.

I give Renée a look. Clearly, he's making money from this.

"Bet Mr. Lebel would love you to get the white streak off his Mustang!" Renée tells him.

"Awww, his Mustang got sprayed? He loves that car." He doesn't really sound all that sympathetic. "I clean interiors, too, for an extra ten dollars." He reaches down, scrubs off a last little bit of white, and the van looks normal again. No skunk streak along its side. He picks up his gasoline jug and straightens up. "Going to vacuum this beauty now. I'll visit Mr. Lebel next. Thanks for the tip."

"You also might be interested in this." Renée pulls a flyer from the backpack. "Tomorrow afternoon the animal shelter is having a Cat-astrophe. Fifty percent off all cats."

"Free neutering," I add.

He takes the flyer and reads. "Great deal! Yup, yup. But I like dogs better."

"What about your mom?" I ask. We often see her sitting outside in their backyard because of the see-through fence between it and the schoolyard.

"She likes cats better. Free refreshments, hmm. I bet she'll want to go."

"Anyone else you know could adopt a pet?" I ask.

"Hey!" He snaps his fingers. "The boss wants to get a kitten."

"Mr. Mason?" Renée says. "But he has a dog!"

"Yup, yup. Says Bailey gets lonely. Dog plays with the next-door cat all the time."

"All right, then." Renée passes him another flyer. "We'll see you there," she says as Ping drags her away.

Pong pulls at me. "See you, Mr. Ron," I call back.

"Bye!" He waves with his big stop-sign hand.

"I know what you're thinking," I tell Renée when we're far enough away that he can't hear. "Mr. Ron could pick up our dog-walking business if we're suspected of burglary and car vandalism ... and he's making money on cleaning off the paint ..."

"Exactly! But he loves cars." Renée sighs. "Same as Attila."

"Yeah. And he does dumb stuff by accident sometimes."

"But painting those cars was definitely on purpose," she says.

"Oh well, looking on the bright side, maybe he'll adopt a cat."

We turn on Duncaster and head up Mrs. Irwin's walkway. The five Yorkies act as an advance doorbell, they bark so much; but I ring anyway, just in case.

She opens the door and frowns at us.

"Mrs. Irwin, Dad finished Goldie's sweater." I hold up the bag.

She reaches for it.

"Can we just come in and see how it fits?" Renée asks.

The Yorkies continue their symphony, and Mrs. Irwin has to hold them back.

"Can you control those dogs?" she asks, looking at Ping and Pong.

I want to ask her the same question, but I step in quickly as she moves to the side.

Renée scoops up Ping and I rein in Pong tightly. The Yorkies mob him, yapping and scrambling over one another to sniff his butt. "Good dog," I tell him as we move into the front hall.

"Wow," Renée tells Mrs. Irwin. "Your house looks exactly like ours. Except you have no dining room wall."

"Had it taken down last week to open up my studio to more natural light."

The Yorkies continue barking until they see me reach into my pocket. Then they all sit, including Pong. "Sorry, guys. Dad did the laundry. No treats in here."

In what would be the dining room at Renée's house, there are paintings leaning against the wall and a huge flat desk with a large, white statue, chest up, of Mr. Sawyer sitting on it. Mrs. Irwin's studio, I guess ...

Mr. Sawyer's bust looks ghostlike, especially the blank white eyes.

Mrs. Irwin crouches down with the yellow sweater. The Yorkies crowd around her now, jumping on her, licking her face. "Goldie!" She snaps her fingers and one of them pushes to the front.

"Mrs. Irwin, who else knew you were making that sculpture of Mr. Sawyer?" I ask.

She struggles to slip the sweater over Goldie. "Besides your father?"

I nod.

"Mr. Kowalski — he was actually hired to do the bust first. But he got into an artistic dispute with Mr. Sawyer."

"Really? You don't find that suspicious at all?"

"If he had the key to my house, perhaps. But he doesn't. Only your father does."

Goldie's head pops through the neck hole and her front legs go through the armholes of the sweater.

"Looks fabulous!" Renée says. "I'm going to *pay* Mr. Noble to make my pet mouse one."

Mrs. Irwin doesn't take the hint. I can't help picturing Mickey in a sweater and I smile.

"Can I just take a photo for Mr. Noble?" Renée asks. "He's going to miss these guys."

Mrs. Irwin nods and arranges Goldie for her picture.

"Say *kibble!*" Renée tells the dog as she aims her cell phone. The other Yorkies try to squeeze in and photo bomb. "Gosh, it must be hard to cope with so many dogs on your own now." Hint, hint. Renée pulls a Cat-astrophe flyer from her pocket and gives it to Mrs. Irwin. "Cats are way easier to manage. You should come to this tomorrow night."

That's where Mrs. Irwin makes a big mistake. Number four of the day. She pretty much admits she can't cope. "I think I'm at my limit of animals."

Renée smiles. "No, actually, you are not. You're over it."

Mrs. Irwin's mouth drops open.

"Burlington animal bylaw clearly states you can only own three of any combination of animals at any given time. Did Mr. Noble not explain that to you?"

DAY TWO, MISTAKE FIVE

Mrs. Irwin turns red and blusters. "They aren't all mine. Two of them belong to my son and daughter, one to my ex. I own two because I thought they needed company."

"Well, as long as Animal Control doesn't know …" Renée says. "Mr. Noble's too nice to ever say anything."

"'Course, if they bark a lot, the neighbours may complain," I jump in.

Raff, raff, raff, raff! The Yorkies sound hoarse, they've been barking so much.

"But if you walk them enough, they should be fine," I tell her, smiling. "Like these two. You should hear Ping before we give them their exercise."

Mrs. Irwin frowns.

"Well, see you, Mrs. Irwin," Renée says.

"Maybe at the Cat-astrophe? Do you want an extra flyer for your children or your ex?" I give her a couple more, anyway, and wave as we step out again with the dogs.

Having used up all their *sit* and *stay* skills, Ping and Pong take off like ponies, and we have to gallop to keep up.

"She can't … possibly … last with them," Renée says between huffs and puffs.

"Slow down, guys!" I tug back on Pong's leash. "You're right. But Mrs. Irwin blames Dad for the missing medal, so no matter what, she's never going to hire him again." I look back for a moment. "We just have to find the real thief." I keep staring. "Say, do you suppose Mrs. Irwin keeps a spare key in her yard, too?"

"Most people do."

"Oh my gosh, Renée. Wouldn't every professional crook know where to find them?"

"Easy to figure out, for sure. Somewhere within ten feet of the door, usually. Plus people give out keys to all kinds of workers, too, and never change their locks."

We speed up again to keep up with Ping and Pong. At the house next door to Reuven's, a squirrel does a front flip into a jack-o'-lantern and the dogs go crazy, Ping barking, Pong straining at the leash.

"He's eating their pumpkin. Should I let Ping go?"

"Never," I answer just as Ping's leash flies out of her hand.

Ping turns into a streak of black and white lightning. He pounces on the pumpkin in a flash. The squirrel's legs tangle in the eye and nose of the pumpkin. At the last minute, the squirrel frees itself and leaps for the brick wall. Ping snaps his teeth on a bit of the fluff of its tail. The squirrel lands and scrabbles up to the roof.

Ping tries the same move, and halfway up, loses grip.

A Pomeranian appears at the large picture window at the front of the house, barking and looking surprised.

The door opens and Red appears, looking just as surprised as his Pomeranian. "Hey, what are you guys doing here?"

"Saving your jack-o'-lantern," Renée shouts back.

Ping, recovered from his landing, zips around the house. Renée dashes after.

"You didn't save anything. He only has one eye now!" Red calls.

"A cyclops pumpkin. Great, eh?" I answer. With Pong leading the way, Red joins me as we follow Renée around the side of the house. Man, I hope she catches up with Ping. Last thing Noble Dog Walking needs is a dog injury, or even an animal assault.

Turns out it's pretty easy. Ping is standing statue-still, staring upward. The squirrel sits on the edge of the roof, twitching his tail and cawing like a crow with a sore throat.

Renée snatches up Ping's leash. Pong moves in beside him, sits down, and also tilts his head back. Renée stares up, too, shielding her eyes, as the squirrel continues to scold the dogs. "Did you know, in California, squirrels rub themselves in dead snake to disguise themselves from live ones?"

"What are you even talking about?" Red says. "You guys are all nutty."

Dead snakes, live snakes. My mind takes a wander. *King, where are you?*

Renée looks down and then crouches beside a bike leaning against the wall. "Hey, Red, did you report this to the police?"

"Report what?" he asks.

She points to the white stripe across his tires, fenders, and frame.

"Oh, *ohhhh*. The white paint mark. No. The bike's old. It's a Reuven find-and-fix-up."

"But was the paint there before?" Renée asks.

"Before what?"

"Before yesterday morning. Someone spray-painted a bunch of cars." Renée squints at him. "Mr. Rupert found the white paint can on your lawn."

"Really!" Red's face turns splotchy.

"Not *his* lawn," I correct her and she kicks me. Ohhh, I get it. She's trying to trip him up and I wrecked it. I backtrack. "I mean, not right smack-dab in the middle of your lawn. More on the border. Closer to Reuven's house."

"I wouldn't know anything about that," Red says.

"What about your buddy, Serge? You know he's been in trouble with the police before?" Renée says.

Yeah, he dognapped Pong! But at the time, he was unhappy about his mom remarrying. She cancelled the wedding since then, so there's no reason for him to be vandalizing cars these days.

Unless something new in his life is bugging him.

"Your brother, Attila, is in trouble all the time!" Red answers.

"My brother creates art! Your friend is a juvenile delinquent." She's holding her backpack likes she's going to hurl it at him.

But this is a mistake. Mistake five. I try to signal her with a finger across the neck, *cut it out*. If Red is the criminal, we need to keep him close, like our enemies.

She rolls her eyes and doesn't notice.

So I change the subject, Renée-style, reaching into the pocket of that backpack. "Have you heard about the Cat-astrophe?" I hand Red a flyer. "We're all heading for the animal shelter tomorrow. There'll be refreshments. And a big sale on cats. Does your dog need a pet?"

"Chip? Why would he need a pet?" He tilts his head, looking a lot like our dog clients.

I grin, confusing him. I am learning from Renée.

"What do you suppose Chip does all day when you're in school?" Renée says. "Not like he can read a good book."

I kick her. "Mr. Mason's picking up a kitty for Bailey," I add.

"For his lunch, maybe!" Red crouches down and pats Pong. "I do like animals, though. It might be fun just to come and look."

"Bring Serge, too," Renée says. "I *know* your friend needs a pet."

DAY TWO, MISTAKE SIX

"We have to be going. Bye." I tug at Pong's leash but he's like an anchored ship. His unblinking eyes still focus upward.

"We'll see you at Cat-astrophe then," Renée says. "C'mon, Ping. Ping? Ping!"

This is the longest the dogs have held still since I've known them. They both sit, unmoving, under the squirrel's spell. Renée finally scoops Ping up. Once she carries him away, I can drag Pong off, too.

We walk just a little way farther, and right next door, we find Reuven outside with a huge stack of newspapers and another pile of sales flyers. "Hey, guys!"

The Frankenstein standing next to him raises his green arms and moans.

Ping leaps from Renée's arms and snaps at it. Pong backs away, growling.

Reuven flips a switch at the back of the monster, then drops down to pat Ping.

I lean over to calm Pong. "There, there, just a machine, and it's off now."

When the animals quiet down again, we begin the job of inserting the flyers into the papers.

As I flip a paper open, Pong drops down, leaning his head across the fold. "Off, off, off!" I push him away and notice the ads for small businesses on that page. One large rectangle shows a diamond, which makes me think of the engagement ring that is not on our client's finger, according to Mom. Why should it be? She broke up with him, after all. I stare at the ad.

Diamond Drywall
No hole too small,
We can fix your wall.

I wonder out loud, "Do you suppose Diamond Drywall takes walls down, too?"

Reuven answers, "It would be way more fun."

"Depending on how busy they are," Renée adds, "they'll probably do anything. Look at Mr. Ron. When the bricklaying work slows, he walks dogs and cleans paint off cars."

"I guess the drywall guy took the wall down in his own house, anyway," I say. Something about that tickles at my brain cells. A thought, fluttering like a fly around a light bulb. Won't land, though. "Did your car get spray-painted?" I ask Reuven.

"You mean the great white heap?"

"Mr. Kowalksi's van, right. That's all your Dad drives these days?"

"Yeah, we no longer own a car. Mr. Kowalski really doesn't drive all that well, so Dad takes him around. Especially on junk day."

"Did the heap get spray-painted?" I ask.

"Who can tell? It's white."

"With white filler in the dents," I remember out loud. "You'd have to look pretty closely to see."

"You can check when we deliver the papers. But why would anyone bother if it doesn't even show?"

Renée and I stop inserting for a moment and look at him. Why would someone spray-paint someone else's car at all is the real question. But Reuven has suggested the answer: to leave a mark. Reuven's knowing that answer seems suspicious.

"It's a nice big canvas," I say. "But you're right. White on white wouldn't be much fun."

Renée changes the subject. "Your dad must have driven the Mr. Universe medal over to Mrs. Irwin's, right? After Mr. K and Mr. Sawyer had that big blow-up about the statue?"

"I don't think so. He told me Mr. Sawyer took the medal back and delivered it to Mrs. Irwin's himself."

"Do you know what they fought about?" I ask.

"Yeah. Mr. K wanted his full name across the statue and Mr. Sawyer thought it would be distracting."

"But the name of the artist on a piece is very important," Renée says. "The name can add value."

"Tell that to Mr. Sawyer." Reuven loads most of the papers onto the wagon, which already sags in the middle. The rest he stuffs in a large canvas bag, the strap of which he hangs over his shoulder.

Reuven chooses to deliver to the left side of the street. Renée and I pick alternating houses on the right. We hand him a bundle of Cat-astrophe flyers.

"Gee thanks," he says. "Something else to carry."

"Do you want a dog to run with?" I ask.

"No thank you," he answers.

"You're welcome." Renée and I jog up to the doors, her with Ping and me with Pong.

I purposely choose to deliver to Mr. Rupert's 'cause I really don't want Renée asking about Mrs. Klein. She was our school custodian and she used to date him. I'm sure Renée would have asked him last night if he hadn't grabbed me and threatened to call the police and all.

Pong dashes up to the house and stands quietly next to me as I ring the doorbell. Mr. Rupert answers. His yellow hair sticks up like short lightning bolts and he folds his arms across his chest like two logs in a fire. "What did you find out?" he asks.

"First of all, here's your Cat-astrophe flyer." I hold it out to him and he has to unfold his arms to take it. "You should really come to this. Maybe save a cat. Also, here's your newspaper." I hand him the *Post*.

Both of his fists hold something now. Good to keep them busy. "So who else knows about Mr. Sawyer's medal?" He repeats this morning's question.

Obviously, Dad, Mr. Kowalski, Reuven, and his father, but I don't want to sic Mr. Rupert onto them. "Honestly, anyone who came to Mrs. Irwin's door. She had her dining room wall taken out and you can see right into her studio."

"Yes, of course. I remember seeing the drywall truck at her house not that long ago."

"Narrow, tall panel truck? White?"

"Diamond Drywall. Sure."

Another totally different thought hits me then. "Mr. Rupert, how exactly did you find out about Mrs. Irwin and the missing medal?"

"What do you mean? I make it my business to know what's going on in this neighbourhood!"

Good enough answer for me. Has to be.

Renée waves from the sidewalk. I move quickly so she doesn't get her chance.

"Don't let that animal defecate on my lawn on your way out!"

"No, sir," I say. "C'mon, Pong. See you, Mr. Rupert."

Not quick enough. Before Mr. Rupert shuts the door, Renée singsongs from the sidewalk, "How's Mrs. Klein, anyway?"

So much for saving him from her nosy questions. If he answers her, the whole neighbourhood will also know.

"Far as I know, she's fine," he grumbles.

"Take a flyer for her!" she calls. "Bet Mrs. Klein would love a cat."

I bet she would, too, and I hold one out to him. But he doesn't take it, which should answer Renée's real question. Both Mrs. Klein and Mr. Rupert are lonely people again. Pong and I leave and grab a newspaper for our next house, which is square and towers over all the others. Mr. Kowalski's.

It has pale-blue siding, a bright-red door, and a railing around the edge of the roof, as if someone paces up there.

I check out his truck while Renée and Ping deliver his paper. There's no trace of white spray. In fact, a line of clean white paint might have been an improvement.

Renée rings the bell, which sounds like a loud gong. Pong and I join her. The door opens, and we can see the crazy-high chandelier in the hallway and all the oversized paintings on the wall.

Hunched over with a paintbrush in his hand, Mr. Kowalski gazes out at us, looking as though he sees something else.

"Sorry, did we interrupt you in the middle of painting?" I ask.

He blinks and wipes at a speck of blue paint on his nose.

"Mr. Kowalski, did you know that a lot of famous artists have pets?" she asks.

"I suppose that's true." His eyes finally seem to focus on us. "Working on your own can get lonely."

"Yes, and Burlington Animal Control has a sale on cats tomorrow afternoon. Here's their flyer. Half off and free neutering."

Mr. Kowalski nods. "Cats don't need lots of attention."

"Or walking," Renée says.

"Wouldn't want to end up with five of them, though. Like that brainless woman with her herd of Yorkies."

"I can't believe Mr. Sawyer hired Mrs. Irwin to make the bust for his medal," Renée says.

"Pompous idiot. He thinks his body is the real art. He constantly flexes and poses. Says I should stop hunching over. As if osteoporosis is some character flaw of mine."

"Is it true he wouldn't let you sign your work?" Renée asks.

"Only on the bottom of the sculpture. Who would lift the bust to see it there?"

"I guess Mrs. Irwin doesn't mind," I say.

"Takes all kinds." He shakes his head and shrugs his shoulders. "Let's see if she even gets paid. He offered to give me bodybuilding lessons in exchange for the sculpture."

"Wow. Bodybuilding lessons from a former Mr. Universe." In my mind, I'm imagining my own skinny body with bulging muscles.

He nods. "I thought it might help my table tennis."

"Too bad it didn't work out." I sigh in sympathy with him. "Well, we hope to see you at the animal shelter tomorrow."

"Only if Mr. Jirad can take me," he answers. "I can't drive at night anymore."

Last time Mr. Kowalski gave us a lift in full daylight, he drove over a curb. Better someone else drive. "Reuven wants to come, so I'm sure his dad will drive you. See you."

He goes back in with his *Post* and his Cat-astrophe flyer, shutting the door behind him.

The dogs tug us back to the wagon for our next newspaper. They know the routine by now.

Renée frowns as we each pick up a rolled *Post*. "I love Mr. Kowalski. He's so over the top about stuff."

"Crazy for supporting the arts, right?"

"Yes, and it makes him a great suspect," she says. "He doesn't care about the law. Only the arts."

"Who does that remind you of?" I ask her.

"My brother, of course. I get it, I really do. If only my father could live with that."

She's turning sad, so I change the subject. "Reuven's way ahead of us. We better hurry. You take that house," I point to one in the distance. "I'll take that one." I've given her a house with cheerful ghosts stuck onto the window and a grinning, waving witch standing on the porch.

Reuven is five houses ahead on the left-hand side. We have to scramble to catch up with him.

Ping and Pong love this: the running, the barking at the cats and dogs in the window, sniffing at the Halloween decorations. Meanwhile Reuven zips from house to house out-delivering us by at least double.

So for us, bringing the dogs is definitely a big mistake. Mistake six. If questioning suspects slows us down, taking the dogs up and down walkways completely turns us into turtles. Plus we're exhausted by the time we end up at the other side of Brant Street in front of Mr. Sawyer's house.

"Well, that's kind of a shock," Renée says.

There's a big FOR SALE sign on Mr. Sawyer's front lawn.

DAY TWO. MISTAKE SEVEN

"He's selling his house," Renée says. "But he works so hard on his garden. Pretty close to Champlain High, too."

I shrug at Renée. "He shouldn't have to clean schools anymore, with all the money he must have earned from Mr. Universe endorsements."

"Hey guys! Deliver the paper!" Reuven calls.

We head up the walk to Mr. Sawyer's together. Renée rings his doorbell, and our two hounds bark, but no human answers.

"So, do you think he's short on money? But why would he have a sculpture of himself made if he's broke?" She purses her lips and rings a second time.

"He wasn't going to pay Mr. Kowalski with money, remember?" I say.

No answer again.

Renée gasps and snaps her fingers. "Maybe Mr. Sawyer's dying."

I shake my head. "Maybe he just wants to move away from Mrs. Watier."

"Yeah. Who wants to live next door to a principal. But he did seem to get along well with her son." She rings one last time.

"And with Mrs. Watier when they dated. Serge will miss him, I bet. Just leave the cat flyer in with the newspaper in the mailbox."

"We won't be able to convince him that way," she argues, but stuffs it in anyway. Houses and properties stretch out here. They have pools and sculptures and water fountains. It takes a while to get next door to Mrs. Watier's house.

In her driveway, we spot a lime-green car with the words *Rottweiler Cleaning Service* in hot-pink letters across the doors.

Renée narrows her eyes. "No one cleans on a Sunday. C'mon, Stephen! This has to be a heist!"

I shrug and follow her. This could be a big mistake. Better just to call the cops if we really think they're robbing our principal. But as we get to the door, it opens, and Mrs. Klein, our former custodian, steps out carrying a tub of cleaning supplies and a vacuum cleaner.

"Well, hi, kids!" Her red curls poke out of a flowered scarf wrapped around her head.

"Hey, Mrs. Klein," I say. "We all miss you at school."

"Isn't that sweet? I miss you, too." She sets the vacuum and cleaning supplies down. "But Rottweiler Cleaning Service allows me to make my own hours. And Mrs. Watier doesn't mind if I clean her house on the weekend."

Renée launches into her campaign without even a beat. "Do you like cats, Mrs. Klein?"

"Love them." Her smile turns sad now. "Mizi passed last year."

"Awww!" Renée reaches out and pats Mrs. Klein's hand.

"Here." I hold out a flyer. "We're all going to the Cat-astrophe at the animal shelter tomorrow afternoon. Lots of cute kitties at bargain prices."

Mrs. Klein takes the flyer and studies it as though it holds the key to the universe.

"Not promising anything, but you-know-who might be there," Renée adds.

She's such a buttinski!

"That's nice." Mrs. Klein sighs. "But I don't think Tom Rupert is ready for a relationship yet."

"He's interested in cats." Renée's eyes sparkle like the frames of her glasses.

Mrs. Klein smiles again but her lips seem all tucked in. "Thanks for this." She waves the flyer as she continues to the lime-green car. "See you tomorrow night."

We grab another couple of papers to deliver and continue on.

Finished with his side of the street, Reuven now doubles back, delivering on our side. When we finally meet up, I high-five him. "We're done!"

"'Bout time. Boy, you guys are slow." Reuven wipes his brow with the back of his sleeve. "Thanks, though. Why don't I buy you both a hot dog?"

Who can say no to a steamed wiener on a warm October day? We head for the convenience store at the end of the street. I wait outside the door with the dogs as Renée and Reuven go inside.

Renée comes out first carrying a large bowl of water for the dogs. The sound of them lapping it up makes me think of gurgling streams. So calming.

I can close my eyes and almost forget that I have lost the Bennetts' key somewhere. That flicker of a memory gets my heart beating double-time.

When Reuven returns holding three foil-wrapped hot dogs close to his chest, I suggest we head for the creek where Attila's latest artwork is sprayed across the inside of that cement pipe. The water will bubble there, and maybe I'll write another message on those rocks. *Keys come back! Criminal, show yourself!* I pat my pocket — drat. Empty, of course. Sometimes I carry a Sharpie.

"Sure. We can stop at the park." Reuven smiles as he hands us our lunch. "Uh-oh, forgot drinks."

A small mistake, I think. I won't even count that.

Renée brings the dog bowl back to the store owner and carries out some sky-blue Slurpees for us. We cross the street again and walk toward that creek.

As we stroll, I sip the frosty liquid in between bites of hot dog. When we reach the potato grater stairs, I'm done my wiener and slide down the slope again with Pong. Renée makes it down faster with Ping.

Reuven stops at the top of the hill and takes off his canvas newspaper bag. "Hey, do you think anyone would steal my wagon?"

Renée squints up at it. "No, it's not garbage day. You're good."

Reuven tosses his bag into the wagon and runs down the stairs.

Renée's eyes narrow when he reaches us. "How did you get white paint on it?"

"Probably from Mr. Kowalski's van. He's borrowed it a few times to move art."

We all sit down on the same flat rock as last time. The water bubbles. I could relax if only the dogs would settle. Instead, Pong pulls toward the cement pipe.

I sigh and stand up. "I'm just going to let him lead me. See what's bugging him."

But of course Ping yanks Renée's arm to join Pong, so she stands up, too. Ping drags her in a zigzag over the rocks, even more twitchy than usual. After all that walking, I can't believe how much the two of them want to sniff around. It's like they're on a squirrel hunt. If the area were fenced, we might drop the leashes and relax, but instead the wagon team pulls us everywhere.

Ping's sniffing leads him to another flat rock that angles over a gap in the ground. The gap makes an overhang, and underneath it is a tiny cave. Ping's sniffing turns into barking, a strange, high-pitched, something-important-is-happening barking. He circles, nose to the ground, more and more frantically. Then he digs near the little cave. Dirt flies onto Pong and he yanks the leash on my arm. Mistake seven of the day turns out to be carrying my Slurpee along on the hunt. The frozen blue slush goes flying.

DAY TWO, MISTAKE EIGHT

"Stephen!" Renée shrieks.

"What? If I wash it right away, the blue won't stain."

"No, look." She points, her eyes and mouth as wide open as the small cave beneath the rock.

I bend down and squint. In that cave lies a coil of hose with black and gold markings. But then a little nozzle head peaks out and a red ribbon tongue flickers, like it's tasting the air.

I yank my head back. "Ahhhhhhh! Snake!"

Reuven comes running. "Pick it up! It's going for the dog!"

"I … I … I …" I become one with the frozen slush on my shirt. "Renée, pick it up!"

"No, you."

"This is King. Our chance to make a new customer happy. Grab him! We don't want him getting away."

Pong dashes in but backs out when the tongue flicks his way. The hose uncoils. The nozzle head swivels toward Ping. Ping moves closer, peeling back his lips and snarling.

Pong definitely carries the brains of the duo.

"Hurry!" Reuven screams. "He's going to bite Ping!"

I can't stand it. Dropping Pong's leash, I dive down and snatch up the snake by the neck. Then

I lift him. He's not even that big. Way shorter than Renée. Feels like leather. I yell, "I'm holding a snake! I'm holding a snake! I'm holding a snake!"

Ping jumps on me, snapping at it. I lift the snake higher. He's not heavy but my arm quivers. The tail of the snake begins to curl up toward my elbow. I want to squeeze really hard till his tail stops tickling at my sleeve. Or fling him high in the sky.

Rouf! Rouf! Rouf! Pong's barking hard, and he never barks, so I know I'm in trouble.

"Don't hurt it," Reuven calls.

Don't hurt it? He's right. I can't hurt King. No matter how I feel about snakes. We need him alive. He's someone's pet, and Noble Dog Walking takes care of pets, even if they slither. "Get away, Ping! Stop that." I nudge the little dog away with my knee. "Renée, grab King's tail."

She shuts her eyes and covers her ears like an explosion is coming. "I ca-ca-can't!" She stomps her feet like she's marching.

"Pu-*lease*, Renée. He's going to constrict my arm!" I hold his head out a full arm's length away. At least he can't choke my neck that way. But the tail begins to wrap around my elbow. "Renée!"

She opens her eyes, drops her head, and yells as she grabs. "Ahhhhhhhh!" Both dogs bark along with her. Renée unwinds a loop of tail from my arm and holds it.

We shuffle toward the stairs. "Can you help us, Reuven?"

"What do you want me to do?" he asks.

"Can you grab the leashes and walk the dogs for us?" I ask.

"You're going to carry that snake all the way to Overton?" He points to my stiff arm raised high above my head. "That high in the air?"

It's starting to feel sore just at the suggestion.

"He's got a point, Stephen," Renée says, holding the tail almost as high. "Our arms are going to fall off by the next block."

"Fine. Call Animal Control!" I shout at Reuven.

"I don't have a cell phone."

"Take mine!" I reach my other hand into my pocket and hurl it at him.

He catches it. "What's the number?"

"Ask Genie!"

He speaks into the phone.

"Hurry!"

He sticks one finger into his other ear and talks over Ping's yapping and growling. "Um, hello. Could you send someone to the little park on Duncaster Road. It's an emergency. We found a ball python."

Renée and I stand there, side by side, frozen, connected by something we hate touching. I don't think I've ever felt closer to her.

I squeeze my eyes so I don't see the little red tongue flicking my way. "How long, Reuven?"

"Um, they're on another call right now. Twenty minutes."

"I can't hold it that long," Renée whimpers.

"Come on, Renée, you just have the tail! Reuven," I yell louder, "I can't hold it that long!" My arm throbs.

"Okay, okay," Reuven says. "I've got an idea."

I hear him pound up the metal stairs and I open my eyes again. He snatches up his canvas bag from the wagon and runs back down.

"Here!" He opens the bag. "Put him in."

I lower the hand holding King. Down, down, down. Close to the bottom of the bag. "I'm afraid to let go!"

"Renée, put your end in," Reuven says.

She lowers her tail-holding hand into the bag, too.

"Good. You're going to let go together. On three. One ... two ... and three!"

Renée and I both release the snake and then jump back. Reuven throws the flap over the top of the bag.

I double over and hang my head and hands down in relief. Then I pick up Pong's leash again.

"We did it!" Renée gives me a hip check.

Reuven is kind of left holding the bag.

But not for long. From the corner of my eye, I see the Animal Control van cruise to a stop at the top of the hill.

"That was fast!" Renée waves to get the driver's attention.

The door opens and a tall woman in uniform heads our way, a net in her hands.

"I thought it might be you kids!" A familiar voice. Janet Lacey scrambles down the stairs. "Nothing much to do at the office, and a truck was free." She ambles over to us. "When I heard the snake call, I thought, I'm *so* there."

"That's okay, we have everything under control. The snake is in Reuven's newspaper carrying bag," I explain. "We can take it back to its owner."

"I don't think so. You called Animal Control and I'm here. I'm taking it in."

Reuven holds out his canvas bag.

She drops her net to take it. "Too bad you guys had all the fun." She takes a peek under the flap. "What a beaut! Did my snake trap actually work?"

"No. We used our bare hands," Renée complains.

Ms. Lacey nods. "Always easiest. So this little guy belongs to someone, but they didn't secure the cage properly."

"Yes," I answer. "Salma Harik. We were hired to make sure her snake ate. But she's away on business till tomorrow."

"Did he get fed?" Ms. Lacey asks.

"Not by us," Renée answers.

"We'll take care of that. You tell her to come over and pick up her pet."

"But she needs to know Noble Dog Walking looked after him properly," I plead with her.

"Yeah, but you're Noble *Dog* Walking, not Noble *Snake* Walking. No way am I letting you hike back to her house with a snake in a bag. He could escape again."

"Are you going to fine the owner?" I ask.

"Depends. How does she feel about cats?" Ms. Lacey asks.

"I don't know." I shake my head. It's hopeless trying to convince her to leave King with us. "Fine. Take the snake to the shelter."

"Exactly what I plan to do … How's Mickey working out for you?" Her eyes twinkle like the diamond on her finger. "You're not returning him, are you?"

"Never!" Renée's eyes narrow. "I'm training him."

"Thought not." Ms. Lacey grins. "But you can't teach an old mouse new tricks."

"Yeah, you can!" Renée insists. "He's walking backward for me."

"Uh-huh. Okay, see you tomorrow." She holds up the bag, smiling at it like a prize. "Don't worry so much. Your client might love a cat."

"Anything would be better than a snake," Renée answers.

"Shhhh!" Ms. Lacey moves the bag away from Renée as though King might hear. "Can I keep this bag for the moment?"

Reuven's mouth shifts, up, down, around, and then up again. "I guess. I'm done my papers for today."

"Good. Swing by the shelter tomorrow afternoon for the Cat-astrophe and pick it up." She waggles her eyebrows. "There'll be cookies." One-handed, she leans over and grabs her net from the ground. "Pick up a cat while you're at it."

Out of my mouth pops a random question, and not the Renée kind. It's a mistake to even ask, I know it. I can't even own one. Because of Mom's allergies. Mistake eight. "Are any of the other animals on sale?"

DAY TWO, MISTAKE NINE

"Funny you should ask that." Ms. Lacey nods. "Minnie just came in this afternoon. Pure white coat. Gorgeous red eyes."

"A mouse?" Renée perks up. "Mickey would love company." She turns to me. "Mice are social animals, you know."

Princess Einstein. "Okay, Renée. But will your dad even let you keep Mickey?"

She shrugs.

"Anyhow, I'm letting Minnie go for free, Monday night special." Ms. Lacey winks. "To the right party, of course." She grins. "Well, I gotta get back to the office" — she holds up the canvas bag — "and feed this here guy."

"Don't use Minnie!" Renée shrieks.

"'Course not. Not before Cat-astrophe. I'll boil King an egg." She heads up the stairs again.

We wave as she drives away.

"She is a little bit strange, isn't she?" Reuven comments.

"A little?" I remember my dream of her marrying the Mr. Universe medal in her office amongst all those cats, and smile.

"Medusa," Renée grumbles.

"Not like anyone else is all that normal in Brant Hills. When you think about it." I want to sit down and talk about all our strange neighbours, figure out the true suspects, maybe figure out the real thief and whether he's our car vandalizer, too. Or she.

But even after delivering newspapers for hours, and capturing and holding onto a ball python for minutes that felt like hours, we still don't manage to sit down. The dogs keep pulling us to sniff around the bushes and rocks. Reuven wanders to the cement pipe, where he gets his first look at Attila's masterpiece. The dogs follow him to see what he's up to.

"Wow!" Reuven raises his hands in awe. "This is such a great likeness of King! Times three!"

Uh-oh. This could be a mistake on his part.

"Attila didn't paint King." Renée folds her arms across her chest. Ping actually sits down now at her feet. "He painted a serpent from his imagination."

"Oh, come on." Reuven points to one of the serpent's heads. "Right down to the colour of his spots?"

Ping yaps at him.

"He never uses live models!" Clearly in a mood now, Renée walks away, dragging Ping.

Reuven knits his eyebrows and turns to me.

Thinking Reuven's attention is for him, Pong flops his tail back and forth against my leg.

I shrug my shoulders.

I know better than to suggest that Attila stole the snake from Salma Harik's house. We did see him just before we entered her house for the first time. Was he carrying something?

I close my eyes and picture Star and Attila, all in black, running across the street with their cell phones in front of their faces. Mr. Rupert's Cadillac screeching to a stop. Yelling at them. I shake my head. So much going on. Whatever. I decide it's best to change the subject. "Reuven, would you have a marker?"

"Certainly. I have one right here in my pocket." He removes a blue Sharpie and gives it to me. "What do you want to do with it?"

"Let me show you." Pong and I lead him from the cement pipe to the stones with the messages written on them. Renée's standing there too, now. Reuven reads some of the messages out loud. "*Harry loves Salma*. Isn't Salma your snake owner?"

"Not a common name. So probably."

"Wonder what this one means. *Ten fifteen, Saturday, October twentieth. Freedom!*"

"Someone had their last cigarette," Renée grumbles.

I bend down to a stone and write, *Find the key*.

"Wasn't ten fifteen the time the power failed yesterday?" Reuven asks.

"Who cares!" Renée takes the marker, lifts a small rock, and holds it at different angles.

"Oh yes, I am certain of it now. Ten fifteen." He shakes his pointer finger at us. "Dad found a perfectly good analogue clock last week. Just had to clean it and plug it in. The hands stopped at ten fifteen yesterday."

I nod. "We were walking Ping and Pong around then." I think for a moment. What could it mean? "Someone found freedom when the power failed."

"Maybe someone quit their job yesterday," Reuven says. "Or could be someone broke up with someone else."

"Harry and Salma! Mom said she was upset on the plane about breaking up."

"Shut up!" Renée snaps.

Reuven and I both turn to her. Is she still this mad because he suggested her brother painted King on the cement pipe?

With her hair covering her face as she bends to write on a fist-sized rock, we can't tell. But the message she puts out to the world is *Happy family.*

Not likely her family is happy if she can't even go home tonight because her parents are fighting so much over Attila.

Is she worried her parents are breaking up?

Her hair falls back, and I see her eyes and mouth all scrunched up as she raises the hand with the rock in it. She pitches it against the cement pipe so hard it leaves a little white mark. The rock tumbles down unbroken. Renée stands there, hands on her hips, mouth and eyes opening back up.

Ping jumps on her leg, barking. She drops down to him and he licks her face like mad. Renée wraps an arm around him.

Crazy little dog.

"I want to do one!" Reuven crouches to take his marker back. He kneels beside a larger stone, tilts his head, and screws up his mouth. Finally, he draws two eyes, two ears, a triangle nose, whiskers, and a circle around it.

Renée looks over, sniffs, wipes at her eyes, and smiles a half-smile. "Awwww. You really want to have a kitty!"

Reuven shrugs. "I like animals."

They both stand up at the same time.

With our goals written on the rocks, I feel a little better. Like we've put them out there for the universe to help us. Kind of how I feel when I count mistakes, like I can separate them from me, analyze them, and benefit from them. It looks like Renée feels better, too.

But then my cell phone buzzes, and I realize it's a mistake to believe a stone can help me solve my problems. Mistake number nine. Especially when the text from Dad reads:

Come home immediately. The Bennetts were robbed.

"Oh no!"

"What's wrong?" Renée leans in to read over my shoulder. She covers her mouth with her hand.

"Reuven, we're going to have to leave you. Ping and Pong's owners must have returned." I swallow.

"They've been burglarized!" Renée blurts out.

"Geez! What does that mean for Noble Dog Walking?" Reuven asks.

"Probably that we'll never be able to walk Ping and Pong again!"

DAY TWO, MISTAKE TEN

We say goodbye to Reuven and try to hurry home with Ping and Pong, worrying all the way as we go. "Do they think we did it?" Renée asks.

"I don't know." I pull Pong away in the middle of a long sniff at a fire hydrant. "Maybe someone saw us searching for the spare key."

Renée allows Ping a five-second sniff at the same spot. "Could be the crook watched us find the secret hiding place." She drags Ping away, too.

"Or maybe someone just smashed a window," I suggest — the best scenario for our family business. "But would anyone have dared going in if the dogs were there?"

"Come on. An extra-long walk for these guys is always a good thing."

"For them, yes. But also for the burglars." Nothing we come up with sounds good for Noble Dog Walking. As we all make the final paw-steps to my house, I suck in a breath. Renée freezes alongside me for a moment.

"Oh no!" She covers her mouth with her hand.

A squad car sits on the street in front of the house.

"This is too much. I can't get in trouble with the police," Renée says.

"Relax. Probably nothing," I bluff. We both know her father will go ballistic if the police talk to him about her as well as Attila. So I babble to comfort her. "They're just going to ask us questions. We haven't done anything wrong." My voice squeaks just a little. Renée's usually the one to calm me down. This is a switch for us and I'm not used to it all. "They can't arrest us. We're kids."

I step inside first, slowly. Pong begins wagging immediately. As we move toward the entrance of the living room, a golden shepherd mix wags back. His face and pointy ears are black like a German shepherd's, but his body looks bright blond like a golden retriever. Did they bring him to sniff out something?

"Renée and Stephen," my dad calls. "Come in and sit down. Constables Jurgensen and Wilson want to ask you some questions about the Bennetts' house."

"Yes." Constable Jurgensen leans forward in a chair — Dad's chair, normally — forearms resting on his legs, his fingers laced together.

Constable Wilson sits tall on the loveseat, smiling at us. "Hi!" She gives a tight little wave. We've met them, and Troy, their police dog, before.

Renée sits next to Dad on the couch, and I squeeze in beside them. Pong circles and finally slumps down at my feet. Ping stays, standing and panting, eyes full only of Troy.

Constable Wilson fingers a loose black hair into the braid tucked in the back of her hat. "Stephen and Renée, right?"

We nod.

"Nice to see you again."

Drifting away from Ping and Pong, Troy nudges Constable Jergensen's hands. He snaps his fingers and the dog sits. Then his antifreeze-blue eyes fix on me, his fingers laced again. "You were just walking the Bennetts' dogs, I understand. Do you mind telling us how you got in?"

"We, um, used a key," I answer.

"You're sure? Your father says he found your key in the dryer."

Of course! Dad did the laundry. I never checked my pockets after. Not for treats or first aid or keys! A big mistake. Mistake ten.

"Did you maybe climb into a bathroom or a basement window?" Constable Wilson winces along with her words as though she understands we didn't mean to do wrong.

"No!" Renée jumps. "We used the spare key hidden on the front lawn."

"Good," Constable Jurgensen butts in. "So why didn't you return it?"

"I did put the key back in exactly the same spot as I found it." I stare back at him.

"I watched him," Renée pipes in.

No one says a word for a moment. The two police officers look at each other. With a few hairs loose again from that braid of hers, Constable Wilson seems more friendly. She speaks first. "When Mrs. Bennett came home, she didn't have her house key. She'd misplaced it. When she looked for the spare, it wasn't in its hiding spot."

"Oh wow! How did she get in?" I ask.

"She called your dad, and luckily, he had your key from the dryer," Constable Wilson explains. "Did anybody see you get that spare key from its hiding spot?"

"Nobody that we noticed," I answer.

Again, the constables look at each other.

"If we figured out where the Bennetts hide their spare key, anyone could figure it out," Renée says.

And she's right. That only makes sense. So how come it feels like we're the ones in the wrong?

"Did you go into her kitchen cupboards at any time?" Constable Jurgensen barks.

Pong's ears twitch. Ping's tail freezes.

"For dog food, sure," I answer.

"You did not, at any time, go into the cookie jar in the very same cupboard?"

"No."

Renée nods her head in agreement.

"Mrs. Bennett had about seven hundred dollars in it." Constable Wilson's bottom lip buckles.

"Who keeps seven hundred dollars in a cookie jar?" Renée can never resist. "Doesn't she believe in debit cards?"

"She says she keeps it to pay workers. They prefer cash," Constable Wilson says.

"It's missing," Constable Jurgensen adds, staring at Renée now.

"Did you check the cookie jar for fingerprints? Because we never touched it," she snaps.

If I let this go and they actually dust that jar, things could go a lot worse for us.

"Um, do you mean the cookie jar shaped like a large Dalmatian dog?" I ask.

"That's the one," Constable Wilson says.

"I may have moved it to get to the next can of dog food," I say.

"You moved it but you didn't look inside?" Constable Jurgensen asks.

"No. I didn't think it would be right to take a cookie without asking," I answer.

One of his eyebrows does a stretch as his lips pull down. He's quiet as his fingers finally unlace. "Well, that's it for now." Constable Jurgensen raises himself up slowly. Troy jumps to his paws, as do Ping and Pong.

Suddenly, we're all standing. The living room feels crowded.

"If you think of anything else ..." Constable

Wilson puts a business card into my hand as she walks past me. "Just call us."

Constable Jurgensen freezes me with one last stare.

Constable Wilson touches the brim of her hat and nods.

And they're gone.

Ping barks one note. The whole room sighs in relief.

"You should have texted me that you couldn't find your key." Dad moves into his own chair, picks up his knitting, and clicks those needles together like a mad fiend.

"I thought I could find it by myself." My feet feel hot suddenly so I pull off one holey sock, and naturally, Ping goes for it, shaking it side to side while one end is still in my hand.

I pull the second one off and Pong latches onto the toe of it. Renée takes over the tug-of-war with Ping.

"What about the dogs?" I ask. "Shouldn't we return them?"

"No. Mrs. Bennett just stopped at home briefly. She's off on another flight."

"You're going to board the dogs even though Mrs. Noble is allergic?" Renée asks.

"The police do not want us in the Bennetts' house for now. And I think the damage here has already been done. Besides, it will probably be the last time they want us to look after the dogs."

"Oh, man," I groan.

Dad nods. "I need pizza," he complains and orders out for supper.

Pizza is relaxing.

Suddenly, Renée drops her end of the sock and hugs Ping. "You're just the cutest dog alive. I can't believe I'm never going to be able to walk you again."

Ping yips. Maybe she's hugging too tightly.

"Why don't you check on Mickey," I tell her in order to free Ping and break up the feeling of sadness. "I'm going to feed the dogs."

She heads up the stairs while I raid Dad's emergency kibble supply. I set out two people-bowls full and make the dogs wait while I count. Only this time, I hold Ping back for an extra three counts. Pong gets a head start. They both finish at the same time.

Renée returns after a bit, just as the doorbell rings. Dad answers, and cheese and pepperoni smells warm the air as he pays the delivery boy. We wash our hands and set the table, and everyone sits down to eat.

"Some good news is that we have an old client back. Buddy, the Rottweiler." Dad bites off the point of his pizza slice.

"Yay!" I punch the air. Ping yips but no one else joins me.

Pong sits quietly, eyeing the mozzarella string Dad wipes from his chin. "The bad news is his owner is paying by cleaning our house."

"That's good news, too. She's a professional. She can get rid of the animal dander so Mom won't get wheezy." Pong slumps down against my ankle.

"She does have a special pet vacuum cleaner. Which is why I invited the canine officer in. No reason the poor dog should stay in the car." Dad takes another bite of pizza, chews, and swallows. "But we really could have used some dog-walking money."

Renée wipes her mouth with a napkin. She's done. Dad and I only eat three more slices ourselves. Nobody has much of an appetite.

The rest of the night we don't talk any more about the robbery or the dogs. For a little while, Renée knits alongside my father in the living room while the dogs and I watch YouTube puppy videos. Then we head for bed, exhausted. Tomorrow's a PA day, so we can sleep in anyway. "Good night!" Renée says to Dad.

"Oh, by the way," Dad says, "your father's coming tomorrow morning with fresh clothes for you."

That's really nice of him, I think. He's never done that before. The dogs and I head off for my bedroom, and Renée heads down the hall for the guest room with Mickey. That's the trouble with having a girl as a friend. No bunking together in front of the TV or in my room.

I set my alarm for eight, since we don't have school tomorrow. Eight should be fine. I lie back in bed. Both dogs leap up to join me. Ping circles three times before settling and I squish up against the wall.

My eyes feel heavy but electricity crackles in my brain. I keep thinking about my tenth mistake of the day. If I had only done my routine pocket check, I would have brought our own key and maybe the Bennetts' house wouldn't have been robbed. For sure, that mistake will cost us my favourite clients. My arm reaches across Pong's warm, heaving body. I might never walk Ping or Pong again. Pong's heart thumps under my wrist. Ping's breath rasps out in a crazy-loud snore for such a small dog. It's like there's a dinosaur trapped in that little rib cage. I love these guys. I have to think of a way to make that mistake right. I'm never going to fall asleep.

day three

THE GREAT MISTAKE
MYSTERIES

But then I do. I wake up before the alarm goes off with hot breath panting on my face. My eyes open to a long snout sniff-sniff-sniffing at me. A tongue takes a swipe at my nose. Wet! I wipe it with a pajama sleeve. Pong. Ping gives a happy yap and paws the blankets off of me.

I jump up. "Guys, I remembered something important!"

Overnight, it's come to me, one strange detail: a brown saddlebag slung over his shoulder. Attila wears black. The saddlebag was the only spot of colour on him that afternoon of the storm when Renée and I bumped into him in front of our new client's house. Is it possible King was curled up in that bag?

My body takes me to the window to check the weather, as I always do in order to dress for the dog walk. The sun's shining, another great day for late October.

How can I even suggest it to Renée? Attila loves lifting weights so he understands the value of the Mr. Universe medal, and he knows all our clients. He likes snakes — he painted the image of King times three on the cement pipe. Maybe it was after he set him loose at the park. Not sure why he'd spray-paint cars, but Attila always seems angry with his dad and the world. Or maybe Star did the car vandalizing. Something to distract the police from the break-ins that involved no real breaking. She was only pretending to look for that can of paint the other night.

I'm standing in front of the window for a few moments before I realize Renée is outside already, sitting in a car in front of the house with her father. Her head's down and she looks like she's crying. Her father reaches to hug her and she falls into his arms. This doesn't look like a clothes delivery at all. Something's up.

I sigh. Whatever it is will not make it easier for me to tell her what I know.

I don't want to disturb their privacy so I lie back down in bed. The dogs jump up on me and immediately try to lick me into action again. I scrunch up my face to resist but it's impossible. Finally, I get back up and dress. They want their breakfast, they need their walk. Our last walk together ever. I sigh.

Unless I can prove to the Bennetts that Noble Dog Walking is innocent. In fact, if we find the real criminal, perhaps the company's value will increase. Pet owners may see us as the true protectors of their animals and homes that we are.

Today is Cat-astrophe day. Will Attila be there with Star? Today, Noble Dog Walking could be vindicated.

I wander back to the window and watch Renée get out of the car and slam the door. Her head is bowed, her shoulders slumped. Her dad gives her a goodbye honk of the horn and I watch a remarkable change come over her.

Renée seems to take a breath, then throws her shoulders back, lifts her chin high, and waves madly, cheerfully even.

Wow. I used to think her cheery sparkle was her most annoying feature. Now I am amazed. She's brave. I want to be that cheery, too, when everything goes wrong. As she turns, I quickly duck away from the window so she doesn't know I've been watching.

"Come on, boys," I tell the dogs. Their ears leap up. "Let's get some breakfast."

Pong pushes me to the side of the doorjamb in his rush to be the first out. Ping ducks under him and dashes down the stairs, barking all the way. Pong tumbles after.

"Hey, Renée," I say gently when we meet on my way to the kitchen.

She smiles brightly. "I have some good news." Ping leaps up to her waist for some attention and she stoops to pat him.

"Really?" I squeak. "Good news?"

"Some." She scrubs behind Ping's ears and he flips over on his back in bliss. "I get to keep Mickey, no worries."

"Your father agreed? That's great!"

Pong muscles in for some pats from Renée, too.

She smiles and strokes his head. "No. I didn't ask him."

"I don't understand."

That's when her mouth buckles and her voice cracks. "Dad is moving out."

"Aw, geez, Renée. I'm sorry." *Happy family*, that's what she wrote on her stone, and instead, her parents' marriage falls on the rocks.

"It's okay," she says, trying to smile again.

I put one arm around her and squeeze her shoulder as we continue to the kitchen. I know it's not really okay but I can pretend along with her. "Let me grill you a chocolate-hazelnut sandwich for breakfast." I decide I won't tell her about my overnight breakthrough regarding Attila.

Dad stumbles in to make coffee and I fire another chocolate special on for him. I think the gooey delicious sandwiches make us feel better. Chocolate helps release endorphins, after all. Renée holds Ping while I feed Pong his kibble, then she releases him and the little dog eats, too.

"This could be our last walk together," I tell the dogs. "Where do you want to go?"

"Wherever you take them, be back by eleven. Mrs. Bennett will be here for her dogs then." Dad slurps at his coffee just a little.

I set an alarm on my phone for 10:45 so we know to head home, wherever we are. Then I head for the door with Renée.

The dogs follow us, Ping barking his excitement. He dodges the leash a few times, teasing me with his terrier humour, but then I settle both dogs down with liver bites.

"Why don't we walk them up to the other side of Brant," Renée suggests as we step out into the October sunshine. "Let's see if we can chat with Mr. Sawyer about his medal."

"All right. We can make sure he looked at his Cat-astrophe flyer, too." Pong and Ping, of course, want to walk in the opposite direction, toward their favourite park. I tug Pong westward on Cavendish, and that helps Ping adjust his thinking.

"We have to announce the criminal at the animal shelter. Save Noble Dog Walking." Renée taps the bridge of her glasses. "And I'm pretty sure I know who it is."

"Really? Do you think Mr. Ron could be robbing houses?" I ask innocently. "He'll take just about any job for money. Crossing guard, bricklayer, dog walker." I'm just throwing random detail at her really, hoping Renée will come up with her brother's name on her own.

"No. Not Mr. Ron."

Ping leaps up on a tree where another Halloween witch has flattened herself in a crash landing. They could use Dad's air traffic control skills.

"Just a decoration, Ping. Give it up." She yanks him along.

I let Pong sniff at it now. "He could have easily picked up Mr. Mason's phone and laptop." Pong lifts his leg but luckily, even at his greyhound height, he can't manage to spray the witch.

"C'mon, they're friends."

"Maybe Mr. Mason didn't pay him enough. Dad told me once that he's kind of a cheapskate. And Dad would know."

At the corner of Brant Street, we herd the dogs together — it's a busy crossing. "Sit!" I raise a finger. "Stay! Wait!" I slip them both a liver bite.

Renée looks both ways. "All clear!"

"Okay. Forward. Go!" I tell the dogs.

Renée starts talking again on the other side. "My feeling has to do with Mr. Sawyer. His moving has me suspicious."

"You think he needs money so badly he'd rob someone's cookie jar?" I ask.

"Seven hundred dollars is not cookie crumbs," Renée says. "If he's desperate for money and he doesn't think anyone will catch him ..."

A loud rattling followed by a crash starts Ping barking.

I turn toward the noise. Serge Watier, our principal's son, is practising his skateboard jumps on his homemade ramp in the middle of the road.

When I notice Red sitting on the sidewalk with his own skateboard tucked under his armpit, I wonder out loud, "Do you find it odd that a high school kid hangs out with someone in grade seven?"

"Yeah. Kinda."

The dogs drag us toward the skateboard ramp where Serge is picking himself up from the road. He wipes his hand on his jeans and I see a dark spot appear there. Blood? He must have scraped it. That's when I pull a Renée move, asking a none-of-my-business question of someone who's probably in a really bad mood. First mistake of the day. "Serge, how do you feel about Mr. Sawyer moving?"

DAY THREE, MISTAKE TWO

Serge stares at me. "I couldn't care less." His stare seems death-ray intense, mainly because he suffers from heterochromia. Renée will happily explain to you that this is a condition causing two different-coloured eyes. His left eye is green, his right is brown. "I don't want to lift weights with Sawyer anymore, anyway," he grumbles.

But grumbling probably means he cares a little.

Pong nudges him for a pat. I can't believe Pong still likes Serge after he locked him away in his pool house for days while waiting for ransom money. Wonder what kind of sentence he got for that, seeing as he's out on the streets now.

"Let me get this straight," Renée cuts in. "You lifted weights with a former Mr. Universe?" She pretends to be wowed, trying to get on his good side, I suppose. Good for her. Keep your enemies close.

"A couple of times. No biggie." Serge scratches behind Pong's ears and hits a good spot. Pong tilts into the scratch. His right hind leg beats to the rhythm of the scratch. "Sawyer has a gym in his basement. He invites lots of guys to work out with him."

"Girls, too," Red pipes in. "I saw that lady, what's her name, with the belly button ring …? The one you have to volunteer with for your community service?"

"Who cares," Serge snaps.

Ping yips. Pong leans away.

I tug the greyhound farther away. "Does your mother lift weights with him?" I actually think that it would make sense for a principal to get all buff in case she needed to handle some really rough students.

"Nah, not Mom. I wish."

"I've lifted weights with him," Red pipes in.

Renée ignores Red. "Do you know why Mr. Sawyer is selling his house?"

Serge shifts his stare to his hand, opening and closing it.

Ping drifts in hopefully; that hand signal could mean a dog treat, after all.

Blood beads up on the scrape. Serge wipes it on his pants before answering. "He wants to open his own gym. Zoning laws say he can't operate that kind of business in this neighbourhood."

"Ahhh!" Renée says as though she's solved the last clue in a crossword puzzle.

"Sure wish they would change those laws," I say. "I would pay to work out with Mr. Sawyer." If I had the money.

Serge frowns down at his hand.

"Say, you should disinfect that wound," I tell him. "You wouldn't want to get flesh-eating disease."

"He's right. We should go to your house and grab a bandage," Red says.

"Shut up," Serge growls and licks the blood from the back of his hand.

"Ew," Renée says.

Pong lifts a long leg against the skateboard ramp.

"We'd better be going." I signal Renée with my eyes and she loosens the rein on Ping. "See you later this afternoon at the animal shelter?" I ask Serge.

"He has to go," Red says. "Part of his community service."

"That must be rewarding," Renée says as Ping dashes ahead.

"Sure," Serge growls.

Pong races Ping, and Renée and I gallop after the dogs. Behind us the rattle and crash starts up again.

Several huge homes down — this is a posh neighbourhood — we spot the FOR SALE sign on Mr. Sawyer's lawn and, surprise, the Diamond Drywall truck in his driveway.

"Perfect," Renée says. "We can ask that guy, what's his name" — she snaps her fingers as it comes to her — "Harry, to the Cat-astrophe, too."

We turn onto the walkway toward the house and see a guy in a grey hoodie and track pants stepping out the door. Hood up boxer-style, he looks pretty fit. His navy track pants sport two stripes on each leg — makes you twice as fast, I think. His clashing neon-pink and orange sneakers scream "athletic" and "colour blind" at the same time.

"Hey, Harry!" Renée calls, which startles both him and me.

She's bluffing. We don't know for sure that he's the drywall guy.

"Hello," he answers back.

Renée's always right, though.

Following close behind Harry is Janet Lacey, wearing a track jacket that's open to a crop top and harem gym pants. In the skin gap between the two, a gold belly button ring glints in the sun.

"Did Ms. Lacey tell you that she has your snake?" Renée asks.

Harry snaps around to look at her. Both of his eyes are coffee black. Not knowing him well, I can't be sure, but he seems annoyed.

"I didn't know you like snakes, Harry. Yeah, the kids and I caught a ball python at Duncaster Park yesterday."

"It's yours, isn't it, sir?" I ask.

"Not exactly. It belongs to my ex-girlfriend."

Ms. Lacey smiles. "I may have to fine her for improper caging of an exotic pet."

Harry's grin opens like a sunrise. "Stupid thing was always getting loose."

"Not the snake's fault," Ms. Lacey says.

"Snakes belong in the jungle," Harry agrees.

"Are you coming to the Cat-astrophe?" Renée changes our line of questioning.

"He's coming as my guest, right, Harry?" Ms. Lacey grabs his arm and gives it a squeeze.

"Yeah, sure, I'll be there. If only to check on my drywall job. But I can't take any cats. Not till I have a place of my own."

"Did you give Mr. Sawyer a brochure, Ms. Lacey?" I ask. "I mean, we put one with his newspaper yesterday, but did you mention it to him?"

"Uh-huh, he is very supportive of the animal shelter," she answers. "He offered to give us all a discount to his gym. When he opens it."

"Do you know when that will be?" I ask. "And where?"

"Nope. He has to wait for the insurance money for his Mr. Universe medal," Ms. Lacey says.

Harry's eyes bug out of his head now.

"Yeah, 'cause insurance takes forever," she continues.

Harry blinks quickly a few times as though willing his eyes to calm down. Too late. His face has made a mistake. Mistake number two of the day is that Harry's face completely displayed his annoyance with Ms. Lacey.

DAY THREE, MISTAKE THREE

On the way back, we pass Serge and Red again. Serge skates up his ramp, grabs some air, and twists around, landing perfectly and rolling back down.

"Now can I try?" Red begs from the sidewalk.

"Go ahead, kill yourself," Serge says. His eyebrows lift and laugh at Red. I don't know what their deal is, but Serge doesn't treat Red very well.

We keep walking but I hear the crash behind us. Ping barks and tries to turn back to attack whatever caused the noise. The wheels, the ramp, the pavement. But there's also a loud "Ow!" I'm guessing the noise comes from Red. I don't have my first aid kit with me, so I can't help him, anyway. Renée has to scoop up Ping to keep us moving.

We wait at the corner of Brant and Cavendish and wave at Mr. Jirad, who is driving Mr. Kowalski's great white heap past us.

My alarm sounds, 10:45 already. We're supposed to be back by eleven. We herd the dogs across Brant Street and down Cavendish quickly, no marking witches or spraying scarecrows or even sniffing hydrants for our wagon team.

We're back at the house by 10:50, but the Bennetts' convertible already sits in our driveway. Renée frowns and shrugs her shoulders. The dogs wiggle and wag; they recognize the car. They pull hard. Really, there's no avoiding facing the Bennetts anyway, so I open the door quickly, step in, and release Pong.

Ping joins him in a beeline to the living room where Mrs. Bennett jumps up from the couch. A tall, thin lady with short white hair and round brown eyes, she could pass for Pong's twin, if she had black spots. She does have super-black eyebrows, a little like the black markings around Ping's eyes, though.

Mrs. Bennett bends down and the dogs swarm her with licks and wags.

"Did my boys have a nice walkie?" she asks and Ping yelps his yes. She looks up at us. "Thank you very much. Your father is just printing up my invoice. Then I'll pay you."

Dad will be happy about this — she owes us for three weeks by now — unless her asking for the bill means she's finished with Noble Dog Walking. But I try not to think like that. Being pessimistic is like being worried about all the bad stuff that probably will never happen. Mrs. Bennett had to pay us sooner or later. Better sooner.

Dad returns with a sheet of paper, which he hands to her. "You can write a cheque or pay by credit card. I have the Square app on my phone. Or send the money electronically when you get home."

She looks at the invoice, nods, and opens her purse. "I'll pay for it now." Even though Dad deducts a little for multiple dog walking, with dog boarding included in, the total has to be close to seven hundred dollars. She can't possibly carry that much cash on her.

But she does. Kind of weird and also dangerous. A mistake, could be number three of the day. She's inviting robbery. She counts it out to Dad, who removes the Noble Dog Walking admin fee and then hands the rest to me. Still over three hundred dollars.

Renée pipes up. "No wonder you got robbed. Do you always carry so much cash?"

Mrs. Bennett straightens. "I have to pay the cleaning lady, and the workers who repaired the wall. I'm afraid the dogs chewed some drywall before we hired your service. Everyone likes cash."

"Drywall?" Renée repeats. "Did you by any chance use Diamond Drywall?" she asks.

"Yes. A neighbour recommended them. Why?"

"Oh, we just met the owner, Harry, is it? We found his missing pet snake and delivered it to Burlington Animal Control. He's going there later to pick it up."

"Yes. Well, I owe him, too."

"Why don't you come, then?" Renée says. "You can pay him and see all the cats up for adoption." She pushes a flyer at her.

"They're on sale," I add. "Free neutering. Maybe you know someone …?"

She glances at it, brows lifted. "A community event?"

"Yes," I answer. "You may not want a cat." I take a breath and take a big leap. "But I think you'll find out who your thief is there." Bold words from my mouth. Are they a mistake? But I need to say something to keep her as a customer, otherwise I'll lose two of my best furry friends.

Some mistakes are worth making.

"Really?" A single eyebrow reaches up in disbelief.

"Really," Renée says. "We are on the case. Noble Dog Walking always has your back. We are … noble!"

"All right." She nods. "We'll be there."

We follow her to the hallway. She leads the dogs to the door. Ping and Pong look back at us as though they can't leave us behind.

"Come on. Let's go home." She tugs them out of the house. When the door shuts, the quiet hits. We all just stand there looking at each other.

Dad sighs. "That's our final payment. Noble Dog Walking has been fired."

I stare down at my fistful of cash. Is this all that's left of my relationship with those dogs? I look up at Renée. She's been with me on every walk, dealing with the craziest dog of the pair, carrying Ping when he wouldn't behave. She deserves half. I count it out and hand it to her.

"Stop, stop!" she protests. "I'm always at your house. You guys feed me. Look after me." Her mouth buckles. Then she snatches the money from my hand and turns to my father. "Here." She holds out the bills I wanted to give her. "You take my share, Mr. Noble. I want to invest it in your dog-walking business. I believe in you. I think animals need you!"

He looks down sadly at her handful of money. From the look on his face, I see that business is even worse off than I think.

Noble Dog Walking forever. I frown and offer my handful of cash to him, too.

Dad's shoulders drop, his head hangs down. "Thanks, kids. This is a wonderful gesture on your part." He shakes his head. "But I can't take your money." He pushes our hands back. "You've actually convinced me. If it's come down to this, I'm taking another job."

Mistake number three: offering Dad our dog-walking money back. We've shamed him so much he's come to the wrong decision.

DAY THREE, MISTAKE FOUR

"Let's head for the kitchen. I'll fix us some mac 'n' cheese for lunch. I'll tell you about it."

Renée and I follow him and pull up chairs.

Dad clatters around in the drawer and then pulls out a pot. He turns on the tap, facing away from me. Over the rushing water, I hear him mumble, "I got a job offer in telemarketing."

If he thinks I'm going to let this little bomb slide by, he's mistaken. Mistake number four. Noble Dog Walking belongs to the whole family, after all.

"No! Dad!"

"Don't worry. I'll be working from home. Calling people for donations to charities." The pot bangs onto the stove. "It's a worthwhile cause."

Tsk. Renée clicks her tongue.

"Just till I wind the business down. And then I'll find something else." Dad turns the stove on and grabs a couple of boxes of macaroni from the cupboard.

I chime in desperately, "Or maybe just till we get some more clients? We can branch out. Become cat sitters. Especially after the Cat-astrophe this afternoon." I raise my hand across an imaginary banner in the air and read from it: "Noble Dog Walking and Cat Sitting."

Dad rips open the boxes and dumps each into the water. I don't even think it's boiling yet. He flattens the boxes with his hands and hurls them into the recycling bag in the drawer. "We have to face it, Stephen. No one will want to sign on with us anymore. I can't give them references. Our former clients think we're house robbers." He shrugs his shoulders. "It's over."

I shake my head. This is the worst, worst, worst thing that's ever happened to us yet. "What about Buddy, the Rottweiler?"

"I can walk him in between calls for now. Oh my gosh. That reminds me, the Rottweiler Cleaning Service is coming this afternoon. We need to tidy up!"

"You're tidying for the cleaning people?" Renée repeats. It's a half-question, half-grumble.

"They have to be able to get to the floors. We've had all these dogs running around." Dad throws open his hands. "Stephen's mom's going to be really sick unless we get rid of every trace of dander and dog hair!"

He's quitting dog walking. I'm still trying to swallow that. It feels like my throat is full of dog hair.

Dad continues panicking about housework. "We need to take off all the sheets from the beds and throw them in the washer. That way, she can vacuum the mattresses, too."

"No worries. After lunch, we'll help," Renée says and gets up to set the table. Dad spoons out the macaroni onto the plates.

I love mac 'n' cheese. It's smooth and creamy. Halfway through, I usually add ketchup and stir, and it turns into a whole other dish, pasta with rosé sauce. But today it's not so smooth. Dad didn't stir long enough and there are tiny clumps of orange powder. I notice Renée giving hers a spin with the fork. I add the ketchup right away. That helps. But it's not the same experience: first half, cheesy, then the second half of the meal rosé. Dad and I usually fight for seconds and thirds. Today none of us finishes our plate.

As we clear up, the landline rings and Dad and I look at each other and smile.

"Mom!" I say.

Dad answers with a cheery "Hello!" He chitchats about the weather and I walk toward him, wanting to hear Mom's voice. He nods at the phone a lot and I reach for the receiver. He holds up a finger to me, as in "wait a minute," while he tells her about finding another job. "Starting this afternoon. Uh-huh, uh-huh." He glances over at me and forces a grin. "It will be great!" he lies.

Then finally, he hands me the phone.

"Hi, Mom."

"Hi, Stephen. How are you?"

"Mom, Dad can't give up."

"I know it's tough right now." She's quiet for a few seconds. Then her voice perks up again. "Sometimes when one door shuts, another one opens."

"Quitting on Noble Dog Walking is just slamming a door. It's a mistake." Number four of the day, but I'm not telling her that. She doesn't like it when I count errors, especially Dad's.

She sighs. "Sometimes, you have to stare at a closed door for a while and watch for the other one to open. Dad's just calling people till the other door opens."

"Mom, I love walking Ping and Pong. Renée loves walking them, too. We'll do it for nothing."

"Maybe you can volunteer to walk dogs at the animal shelter. Isn't this afternoon your cat thing? You can ask then."

"It won't be Ping and Pong."

"Of course not. But maybe other animals need your love and attention even more."

"Maybe."

"Listen, Stephen, I heard something interesting that might help you till that door opens."

"What?"

"British Airways now offers its passengers an all-pets video channel on their entertainment app. Paws and Relax, it's called."

"Really, Mom. How does that help anyone?"

"Watching these pet videos has been scientifically proven to lower the heart rate and reduce stress. Great for anxious passengers."

"So should I hop on a flight to London?" She knows I'm afraid of flying, so how crazy would that be?

"What a great idea! On my standby discount. A little family holiday wouldn't cost much …"

I interrupt her. "But that's with *your* airline. How does Paws and Relax help us, then?"

"It doesn't. What I was actually suggesting was that if you're feeling stressed, watch animal videos."

That mouse training YouTube channel did make Renée and me feel good. Ping and Pong and I liked watching puppies, too. "Thanks, Mom." Even to myself, my voice sounds draggy.

"I'm sorry, Stephen. Things have a habit of turning out the way they are supposed to."

In the background I hear voices.

"Stephen? I have to go. See you tonight. Love you!" *Click!*

"Love you, too, Mom." She can't hear me, the line's dead. But I hope she feels it over the thousands of miles. I hang up the phone.

We don't have a choice. We have to prove to Mom and Dad that giving up on Noble Dog Walking is a mistake.

DAY THREE, MISTAKE FIVE

"Right, well." Dad rubs his hands together. "We better get started on the tidying."

"So boring," I grumble and pretend to snore.

"Just a quick pickup," Dad says.

"I'm falling into a coma thinking about it."

Renée kicks me. I know I'm being a brat. Why should I be nice? Nothing is going my way.

"Should take fifteen minutes." He fiddles with his cell phone. "I'm setting a timer."

I do like a challenge, though.

"You ready? On your mark, get set, and … go!"

The kitchen chairs scrape across the floor as we all push them under the table at the same time.

Renée rushes off for the guest bedroom and I pound up the stairs after her. The race begins. Books, I pile on my desk, my backpack and shoes get pitched into the closet, the door gets kicked shut as I rip off the sheets from my bed and collect up all the clothes from my floor and desk. Then I meet Renée at the top of the stairs and we run down to the laundry room. Dad puts his sheets in, too, adds the detergent, and starts the machine.

"To the living room!" he commands, one finger in the air.

Back up the stairs we run, down the hall. Renée and I clear the end tables of books and magazines. Dad squirrels away his knitting gear in the hall closet. We're just about done when Dad's phone alarm sounds, followed by chimes from the doorbell.

"Right on time," Renée says.

I glance through the living room window. "Rottweiler Cleaning Service has arrived." With a rectangular bucket of cleaning supplies in one hand and a vacuum cleaner in tow in the other, Mrs. Klein stands waiting.

I head to the door and open it. "Hi, Mrs. Klein."

"Can I ask you a question?" Renée calls, stepping into the hall.

Boy, Renée doesn't even let Mrs. Klein step in.

"Shoot," Mrs. Klein says as she walks into the foyer, vacuum nozzle pointed our way.

"Did you ever clean Mrs. Irwin's house?

"Oh yes! And that is some job! Dog hair … paint splatters … canvases everywhere." She sets down the vacuum cleaner and her bucket of supplies.

Renée's eyebrows twitch. Does she think of Mrs. Klein as a suspect? After all, Mrs. Klein did lose her job as school custodian. Maybe she's broke and angry about it.

"Well, then. Did you ever see the Mr. Universe medal?

"Nah. I only saw a model of it at Mrs. Irwin's house." Mrs. Klein takes off her coat and opens the closet to put it away.

"But that was the real one," I say.

"No. It couldn't be. It wasn't real gold. I dusted it; I know." She hangs up her coat and turns to us.

"Did you bite it with your teeth to test?" Renée asks.

"Are you kidding? Do you have any idea how much a root canal costs? I noticed some grey metal where the gold plating had worn off."

"Wow. Really. Wonder if anyone else knows?" I say.

"Mr. Sawyer must," Renée says.

"I'm sure." Mrs. Klein moves into the living room with her vacuum cleaner. "Can you show me where the plug is?"

Dad joins us and connects the vacuum cleaner for her.

"Mrs. Klein, can you move my pet mouse Mickey to Stephen's room when you're vacuuming the guest bedroom? I don't want the noise to scare him."

Mrs. Klein's eyes pop. "A mouse in the bedroom? That's not very hygienic."

"It's just temporary. I'm taking him home after the Cat-astrophe. You're still coming, right?"

"Absolutely," she answers. "I'm not hiding from the world."

"Why don't you take Mickey to your house now," Dad suggests. "Stephen, you can go with her. That way you won't be in Mrs. Klein's way."

"Where are you going?" I ask.

Dad frowns. "I'm heading into the garage to start making phone calls. Looking for donations for the Make a Wish Society."

If only they would make my wish come true. I shake my head. "You're really going to set up a call centre in the garage?" A continuation of mistake number four, which was slamming the door on dog walking.

Renée folds her arms across her chest. "Mr. Noble, I think I know who the criminal is," Renée says. "If I'm right, and we nab him tonight, will you at least try to keep Noble Dog Walking running?"

Dad smiles just a little, then tousles her hair. "It's not just finding out who the criminal is. Our clients have to have faith in us. They need to sign back on with Noble Dog Walking."

"But if we can announce the criminal at the animal shelter and everyone hears, they should trust us again and come back, right?"

"Absolutely. Unless they've all found ways to manage without us." Dad waves his fingers at us and heads for the garage.

Renée packs up her clothes and brings Mickey's cage down to the ground floor.

Before we leave, Renée sticks her head out the door. "Do you think he'll be warm enough?"

I stick my head out, too. The air feels damp but not icy. "He should be fine. But just in case … wait here a sec." I zip back into the kitchen and grab an old towel from the broom closet. Then I return to the front door and drape it over Mickey's cage. "I can carry him for you."

Renée opens the door.

Walking without dogs feels so weird! It takes a lot less time to cover territory, though. "Will you look at that? Mrs. Whittingham's put her creepy Halloween display back up." A doll with purple circles under her eyes and drips of blood painted down her chin sits in the swing on her tree. Some tombstones with corny sayings. *Here lies Cale, died from a rusty nail.*

Raff, raff, raff, raff, raff. Oh my gosh, what a racket! I turn from the display to see Mr. Ron in a tangle of Yorkies on the other side of the street.

Rose, Hunter, Goldie, and Blue wear the sweaters Dad knit for them in the red, green, yellow and, well, blue, to match their names. Only poor

Violet wears none. With Mr. Ron walking these guys, I wonder if Dad will even get a chance to knit hers now.

Mr. Ron doesn't notice us but the dogs do. They wag and jump and pull toward us. Head down, Mr. Ron struggles with their leashes, stumbling over them as he tries to walk.

"Hi, Mr. Ron!" Renée calls.

He sees us now and raises his hand to wave. Unfortunately, he drops a couple of leashes at the same time. Blue and Rose break away and cross the street to us.

"Catch them!" he calls.

"Oh no!" Renée cries out.

The Diamond Drywall truck barrels around the corner, heading our way.

She jumps into the street and tries to scoop them up. They dodge her and bow, thinking it's a game. I drop Mickey's cage and wave my arms desperately as I step out into the street, hoping to stop the truck.

Mistake five has to be Mrs. Irwin's for hiring bumbly old Mr. Ron to walk her herd of dogs.

Or will it be me, jumping into the street? The truck keeps coming.

DAY THREE, MISTAKE SIX

It doesn't even slow down.

Renée snags the dogs' leashes and pulls them toward the sidewalk. I push them along from behind with my feet. They bark and nip at my shoes. It's still a game for them.

The truck races closer.

"Move!" I yell at the dogs. But they don't.

At the last possible moment, the truck veers around us. Then keeps going.

Safe! Oh my gosh.

Mr. Ron shakes one fist in the air. "I oughta report him!" It's what he always threatened to do back when he was our crossing guard and someone didn't slow down and obey his stop sign.

"Hold on to those leashes!" Renée calls back to him.

Immediately, he drops his fist and grips the loops with both hands. "Thank you! Thank you," he calls to us and checks both ways before crossing the street with the other three Yorkies. He huffs and puffs as Renée hands him the leashes. "You kids are heroes in my book."

"You're stealing my father's business," I snap at him.

"Lookit. I'm sorry." He shrugs his shoulders. "I have to support Mom and me. I can't say no to money." He tries to detangle all the dogs. Rose and Hunter jump on Mickey's cage.

"Down!" I command, pulling one of Dad's liver bites from my jacket. Instantly, all five sit pretty.

"Hey, can you sell me some of those?" Mr. Ron asks.

I reach into my pocket and dump all I have into his hand. Not like I'm going to need them anytime soon. "Samples," I tell him. "A bag will cost you fifteen dollars."

"I'll buy a bag. *If* I spend any more time with these guys," Mr. Ron says.

"Maybe you should leave the dog walking to my dad," I tell him.

"It's not my fault Mrs. Irwin doesn't want to use Noble Dog Walking anymore," he answers.

Hmph. So there it is. Dad is right; we need to gain our clients' trust back somehow.

"When you come to the Cat-astrophe this afternoon, be sure to tell Mrs. Irwin what heroes we are," Renée says.

Sometimes, it's like she reads my mind.

"Yup, yup, yup. Will do."

Cage in hand, I move away so the Yorkies don't bother Mickey.

"He'd do anything for money," Renée repeats as we start walking. "Stealing a gold medal or taking cash from a cookie jar would be easy compared to walking those Yorkies."

"You're right. But if he robbed houses, he wouldn't bother walking those crazy dogs!" I answer. "A lot of people in this neighbourhood need more money. You heard Reuven. My family, too. Maybe that's why clients suspect us."

We continue past Reuven's house. Frankenstein grins at us, but does not moan, groan, or lift up his arms. Past Mr. Rupert's, we meet Star and Attila coming our way, hand in hand, all in black except for the white skull and crossbones on Star's leggings.

"You don't have a PA day today — you're supposed to be in school," Renée snaps.

I've never seen her so angry with her brother before.

"Relax. It's lunch hour," Attila says.

"Two thirty?" Renée asks.

He smiles and shrugs. Neither of us believes him.

"You're the reason Dad left," Renée says.

"That's harsh," Star says.

"If he didn't keep getting in trouble, Mom and Dad would get along!" A tear leaks down Renée's cheek.

Attila must see it, too. "Aww. Sorry, Renée. Really. But I am who I am." Then he shrugs and opens up his arms. This is a side of him I've never seen before. He reaches for her and hugs her.

"What's in the cage?" Star asks me, maybe to change the subject and pass the time as they hug. She lifts the towel. "Oh. So cute. It's a mousey. Hey, little guy, come on out."

Mickey huddles into his paper towel roll, refusing to make another appearance. Smart mouse.

"Listen, Dad's a perfectionist," Attila tells Renée as they break apart again. "You know that. If it wasn't me doing crazy stuff, he'd pick on you."

"Hey, do you still have that hamster ball we used for the high school art project?" Star interrupts.

"Somewhere," Attila answers. He knits his brow for a moment, then it lifts as though he's found the answer. He points his finger at Renée. "Go down into my room and check on the shelf of my closet. If it's not there, it might be under my bed."

"Thanks." Renée sniffs.

"No worries! Hey, at least you get to keep your little pet."

Renée gives a half-smile and we move on in the opposite direction from Attila and Star.

We haven't walked very far when I spot movement from the corner of my eye. Mr. Kowalski is jogging along the opposite curb, all hunched over, as usual. With his head down like that, he doesn't seem to see us or even the car parked ahead of him.

"Ow! Ow!" He slams into the bumper and rubs his right knee. Then he kicks the back tire with his right foot. "Stupid car!"

"Hey, Mr. Kowalski, are you okay?"

He kicks the tire again. "Double-car garages, and everyone parks in the street!"

"Maybe they're just visiting!" I call to him.

Mr. Kowalski jogs around the car and continues on.

I look at Renée. "Dad's car didn't get sprayed and he parks in the driveway."

She nods. "The great white heap did not get painted, either."

"Even if it could have used it," I add. Mr. Kowalski parks his van in the driveway when Mr. Jirad's not driving it.

"Mr. Kowalski is a lot like Attila. He doesn't let the law get in the way of his art, either." I mention Attila and the law in the same breath, and that's a mistake. Renée always insists her brother is innocent of any wrongdoing. Should that count as number six of the day?

Renée's eyes sharpen but she keeps on walking.

"I don't mean your brother's the criminal this time." We turn off onto the driveway in front of her house. "We have a lot of suspects. I'm sure Attila did not break into any houses to rob them," I lie. I am so not sure.

"Attila cares about art and cars. He doesn't care about technology or money!" Renée's mad at me, despite my lie. She doesn't look my way as she unlocks her house door. She throws in her backpack of clothes, then holds out her hand. "Give me Mickey."

"I'll carry him. I want to see him in that hamster ball. Hey, I could video him and we could post that

on YouTube." I'm babbling. I just don't want to leave
Renée mad and upset about her brother.

"Fine, let's check out Attila's room. See if we can
find the ball."

We take off our coats and shoes. This will be the
first time we've really hung out at Renée's house.
Feels a little strange. It's super quiet, the floors and
walls are grey, and the furniture that I can see from
the hall is chrome and glass and white, cool and
frosty like icebergs in the Arctic. No wonder Renée
never wants to stay here alone.

We leave Mickey on the floor in the hall and
head downstairs for Attila's room, which is the one
place I *have* been in Renée's house. It's huge and
the bed is king size with fuchsia-coloured bedding
all neatly made. Hanging above it is a large picture of a cleaning lady in uniform, dustpan in one
hand, lifting a wall covering with the other. *Maid
in London* by Banksy, which is the pen name of
Attila's street artist hero. No one knows for sure
who he really is.

"You check the closet. I'll check under the bed,"
Renée says. Makes sense since I'm the tall one.

I open the door and the clothes in there are
hung evenly spaced, arranged by shirts and pants
and colours, mostly all black but some brown.
One pair of khaki pants hanging alongside all the
black looks bright by comparison. At the top of

the closet sits a black fedora hat, an eight ball, and several orange and yellow Nerf guns piled on top of each other. "No hamster ball here!" I close the door and turn.

Mistake number six has to be Attila's, having us search through his room when he has something serious to hide.

Renée sits on the carpet, open-mouthed, with her eyes widened into full moons. She's holding a small notebook computer in her hands, opened to a screen that's cracked in a really interesting pattern. The computer is bright red.

DAY THREE, MISTAKE SEVEN

"Mr. Mason would never own a red laptop, would he?" she asks.

"Actually," I answer, "he told me both his phone and his laptop were red. He said it was so he could find them better. But his truck is red, too. I think he just likes the colour."

Her shoulders slump. "So Attila took his laptop. Where's the phone, then?" She lifts the duvet and peers beneath the bed.

"Come on, the laptop is broken. Maybe he scavenged the garbage like Mr. Jirad does on junk pickup day. Found it there." In my mind, I see Attila going to hurl his cell phone because some game he was playing didn't work. Star stopped him. Maybe she wasn't there to do that this time.

Head sideways, Renée squeezes under the bed and slithers around like a snake.

"Maybe you should just leave it alone!" I look under the bed myself. Not even dusty. Gotta hand it to Attila; he sure is neat.

"Found the hamster ball." Renée whacks it out and I catch it. It's clear plastic with air slots, just slightly smaller than a soccer ball.

She keeps slithering. "No phone anywhere. Maybe he pawned it already." She shimmies backward out from under the bed. When her head comes back out, she sits up.

"You said he doesn't care about technology or money."

"But he loves snakes." Renée's lip buckles. "Bet if we hadn't found him first, Attila would have moved King in here, now that Dad's gone." It does not make her happy to suspect her brother, and even though it's always easy to make him for the criminal, I want to cheer Renée up.

"Oh, come on! He didn't steal King to keep him in the park just in case your father left."

Renée frowns at me. "No?"

Trouble is, saying it out loud actually made it sound plausible. Every day, Attila was painting inside that cement pipe with his new pet snake to keep him company, maybe to even act as his model.

Her eyes look like they're going to swallow me up. Even the sparkles from her glasses seem to challenge: *Prove my brother innocent!* And I want to, really I do, but I remember that brown saddle-bag over his shoulder the night we first went over to feed King. The bag that could have easily fit one small ball python.

Renée's father left her family this morning; my dad gave up on our dog-walking business this afternoon. Doors are slamming shut all around us. We need something to make us feel better.

That's when I remember my mother's story about British Airways' Paws and Relax video channel, which we all could use right now. Or at least the closest thing to a cute animal video channel. Just till some door opens somewhere. I pick up the hamster ball. "Hey, Renée, let's try Mickey out in his new toy!"

She sniffs and nods, pushing the red laptop back under the bed.

I offer her my hand and pull her up. Then we head upstairs back to iceberg land and kneel down beside Mickey's cage in the hallway.

I unlatch the cage door, twist open the ball, and lean it up against the door. Mickey's shiny black eyes stare as his little pink nose twitches. Seems like he can't believe his eyes or his nose. It takes a few moments for his curiosity to build into courage. Finally, one long-fingered pink hand reaches over the rim of the plastic ball, then the other. He scrambles in and Renée closes it. She sets the ball on the floor.

At first Mickey wanders and sniffs, satellite ears listening for danger. Then he walks in one direction, which makes the ball roll a little. He pauses for a moment, then walks a little faster in the other direction. *Clunk,* into the wall. He tries again. When he notices he's getting somewhere, he breaks into a full-out mousey jog. Along the wall, down the hall. We chase after him. Faster! He's like the greyhound of mice. Into the kitchen, the ball clunks into the chair and table legs. He slows down. Around and through, back and forth.

Finally, the wheel wedges up against the fridge. Mickey stops and sniffs.

"Maybe he's hungry," I suggest.

"Take him for a moment," she says.

Gently, I pull the ball away. Renée opens the fridge, rummages in the crisper drawer, and brings out a baby carrot.

She opens up the ball and gives it to him.

Mickey takes it into his little pink hands, whiskers twitching. Nibble, crunch, nibble, crunch. He loves it.

How can the world be so crazy when a vegetable tastes so delicious to Mickey?

Renée and I both smile. Paws and relax works.

My phone buzzes and I check for a text. "It's Dad," I say. "He wants to leave soon for Cat-astrophe. Be there early."

"I wonder why," Renée says.

"To get the best cookies?"

"I don't think so. I bet he wants to meet everyone so he can get new clients! Your father's not giving up after all!"

"Maybe!" I agree as I stand up. "You wanna come with us?"

"Sure," Renée answers. "Just let me put Mickey in my room." She grabs the ball and sets it so that Mickey will climb back into the cage. Mickey's still too busy crunching down on that carrot.

Then the front door opens and the smell of barbecued chicken wafts through the air. "Is that you, Renée?" Before Renée can answer, Mrs. Kobai steps into the kitchen carrying several bags of groceries in each hand, one of which produces that irresistible smell. She hoists the bags onto the counter and points to Mickey's cage. "What is that?"

"My new pet. You always said you would let me have one if I could get Dad to agree."

"A fish ... maybe a cat?" Mrs. Kobai shakes her head and folds her arms. "But I thought we would discuss it first."

I jump in, hoping to rescue the situation. "Mrs. Kobai, I'm sorry Renée didn't ask you before bringing

Mickey home. She never planned on adopting him. She was actually saving him from a snake."

Mrs. Kobai stares our way for a moment, her eyes big the way Renée's sometimes get. Then she sniffs. "Your father leaves and you replace him with a rat?"

Renée's eyes fill. I didn't rescue anything. But mistake number seven certainly goes to Renée for assuming her mom would allow her to keep Mickey without asking her first. Not everyone is good with rodents, after all. Allergies aside, I'm not sure if my mom would be, either.

I try to save the situation again. "It's a mouse, Mrs. Kobai. And Renée's already trained him to moonwalk."

Mrs. Kobai shakes her head and closes her eyes. It's not looking good for Mickey. Then she sighs and opens her eyes again. "Go wash your hands with lots of soap. Then you can set the table. Stephen, are you staying for supper?"

DAY THREE, MISTAKE EIGHT

If I leave, will there be a big argument? Will Renée say something annoying to her mother, and then will her mother say, "Take that animal back to the pound!"?

This is what I worry about. Renée's already sad enough about her father leaving, and about her brother possibly, maybe even probably, being a thief. I want to stay for her sake. I know her mother really wants me to leave. It's awkward.

"Sorry, Mrs. Kobai. My dad just texted me. We're going to Cat-astrophe right now. Renée was planning to come with us."

"Not now!" Mrs. Kobai says. "After supper," she tells Renée.

I want to say something else, maybe explain how animals can make you feel better and that Renée needs to feel good about something. Tell Mrs. Kobai about Paws and Relax on British Airways.

But looking at Mrs. Kobai's frown just makes me feel bad for her, too, so I don't.

Mickey finally climbs out of his ball and into the cage. Renée shuts him in.

"Well, then. See you later." I grab my coat and head out the door.

Walking without a dog or a friend has to be the most boring thing to do in the universe, especially since I've seen all of the Halloween decorations a few times already. All I can do is try to squeeze my brain like a lemon for fresh juice on the crimes. All fingers point to Attila, but just like every really good detective story, I want the criminal not to be the person everyone suspects. I run through other possibilities in my brain.

The criminal could be Mr. Kowalski, I think, as I stroll past the car he kicked. Cars parked in the street interfere with his jogging path and he would definitely spray-paint them if he had a can handy. He's also mad at Mr. Sawyer for firing him from the sculpture job. I bet he'd steal that gold medal and trash it just for spite. But I don't think he needs Mr. Mason's laptop or phone, or even Mrs. Irwin's money, for that matter.

I stroll along a little farther and spot a bag of dog doo near the sidewalk. I roll my eyes. Red used to put his Pomeranian's poop bags in trees. Is this his handiwork? He skateboards a lot with Serge these days. Do the cars in the street bother them the way they bother Mr. Kowalski on his jogs?

I shake my head at the sight of that little black-knotted bag. Do we still have to be responsible dog people even if Dad gives up his business? But maybe, like Renée says, he's going to keep it. Especially if we find the real thief. We have to find him!

I bend down and scoop up the bag.

Maybe bumbly old Mr. Ron dropped the bag as he struggled with all the Yorkies. Would he steal a phone and laptop if he were mad at his friend-turned-boss about giving him too much busy work? Did he want to be a dog walker so badly he broke into all our customers' houses to take the business away from Dad? But how would he know there was money in Mrs. Bennett's cookie jar? Or that Mrs. Irwin was storing that supposedly valuable Mr. Universe medal in her house? And why would he bother about the snake at all?

A tall white truck whizzes by, always too fast for this neighbourhood: the Diamond Drywall van. Harry, the weightlifter, did some drywall work in both Mrs. Bennett's and Mrs. Irwin's houses; he probably knows all the hiding places for keys. Maybe even made copies of them. But then, Rottweiler Cleaning Service could do that, too. It's so unfair that everyone blames Noble Dog Walking for these thefts.

When we told Harry about finding King, he said flat out that snakes belong in the jungle. Does he consider Duncaster Park the jungle, I wonder?

Oh my gosh, will he even tell his ex-girlfriend Salma that her snake is waiting for her at the animal shelter? I'll have to write her a note. I'll ask her if she's missing a diamond ring from that bell box in the freezer, too. Maybe the criminal will try to pawn both the Mr. Universe medal and the diamond ring at the same time.

I wonder if Salma is a bodybuilder like Harry. Did she train with Mr. Sawyer, too?

What about Mr. Sawyer himself? What did he do with the real medal? Did he sell it already? Maybe he stole the fake medal for the insurance money so he could open up his gym. Does he like snakes, I wonder? How does he feel about cars parked in the road?

At Mrs. Whittingham's house, I slow down to see if she needs help with anything. Looks like she's loading up the daycare kids to take home for the day.

She puts her purse and diaper bag on the roof of the van, then she slides open the door to lift in an infant car seat. Her son August and the rest of the kids must already be inside the van. Seems like she watches about ten of them at her house. She closes the door and blows her hair from her face. She doesn't need me — she has everything under control.

I wave to her and she waves back as she wipes her brow with her other arm.

She opens the driver door, climbs in, and shuts it.

Wait a minute. The diaper bag and purse are still on the roof! "Mrs. Whittingham," I holler. "Mrs. Whittingham!"

She doesn't hear me. Instead, she backs up the van.

"Stop!" I run closer, waving my arms like mad. The windows are closed. Maybe she's playing loud music or the kids are all talking, but she doesn't hear me. She's about to make mistake number eight of the day.

As she turns onto the street, the diaper bag and purse slide from the roof at the same time.

Mr. Rupert drives up in his big green Cadillac. His trumpet-note horn sounds loud, like it's coming from a train. Finally, something gets Mrs. Whittingham's attention. She stops the van.

I pick up the purse and bag from the pavement and hold it up for her to see.

She puts her head down on the steering wheel. I bring them to the driver's side. The window glides down.

"The bottle's not even broken." I hand the bags to her.

"Thank you, Stephen!"

"You're welcome. My dad once left his favourite coffee mug on the car and drove away. Not the worst mistake you could make." Something my mom often says to me.

Mrs. Whittingham smiles at me. Across her forehead is the faint mark of the steering wheel.

"Say, did you know? The animal shelter is having a Cat-astrophe today," I tell her. "Free refreshments. All cats must go. August might like a kitty."

She takes a deep breath, then blows it out. "I don't need one more thing to look after. Bye!"

DAY THREE, MISTAKE NINE

Walking on, I realize my big mistake in not staying with Renée for supper. First, there's the barking, high-pitched and desperate. Then I see them through the picture window of the Bennetts' living room. The black and white wagon team. Mismatched as they are, I love them. The least I should have done is walked on the other side of the street, the way we did on the way over. Perhaps they wouldn't have seen me.

Ping jumps up and down and Pong silently wags, brown eyes fixed on me. I feel my heart thumping slower and harder. My throat swells up so I can hardly swallow. Suddenly, they disappear, which makes me worry. I stop and wait. What could have happened to them?

The door opens and the question is answered as Mrs. Bennett steps out with the dogs on their leashes. They're not behaving at all for her and I've given away all my liver bites. Another mistake. Gah! Ping jumps along on his hind feet, barking at me. Pong does a merry-go-round move that tangles the two leashes.

I can't help myself. "Can I take one of them for you, Mrs. Bennett?"

She shakes her head no, but by now, Pong has wound the leash around her so tightly she can't move. I grab the handle from Mrs. Bennett and unwind it. She's free.

"Thank you. I can take it from here."

"I don't mind. We're heading the same way." I'd have to cross the street in order to avoid Ping and Pong and their circus act.

"All right." Ping pulls Mrs. Bennett so that he can rub his body along a cedar hedge. Behind him, Pong lifts his long leg against the fire hydrant.

Usually, Ping would double back to mark the same spot as Pong, but instead he burrows into the corner hedge. His body turns stiff, his tail becomes a straight arrow. His back legs quiver.

"He might have a mouse or something," I tell Mrs. Bennett.

She crouches down and pulls him out by his little haunches. Sure enough, he's chomping on something.

It's small and rectangular and red.

Mr. Mason's phone?

Mrs. Bennett kneels on the ground and sticks her fingers in the corner of Ping's mouth to apply pressure. His leathery black lips part to show his white teeth in a death grip.

"Ping!" I stick my hand into my pocket, which is totally empty. But he doesn't know that. Instantly, he releases the phone and sits up tall and straight, ears out like airplane wings.

Mrs. Bennett picks up the phone.

"Good dog!" I tell Ping and reach down to pat him. He noses into my hand and licks it frantically. "Sorry, nothing there."

"What a strange place to drop a cell."

"Oh, I don't think anyone dropped it. Does it work?"

She presses some buttons and shakes her head. "Perhaps the battery's just run out."

"I know who it belongs to. He'll be at the animal shelter this afternoon. Do you want to return it or should I?"

"Here you go," she says. "I'll take Pong, now. The two of them seem to have settled down."

We swap the leash for the red cell, which I slip into my pocket, making sure to button the flap to keep it in. Then I take my cell out of my other pocket and text Renée. *Bring the broken laptop to Cat-astrophe. I know who took it.*

Mrs. Bennett walks ahead but Ping and Pong continue to look back for me.

"See you later!" I call.

Instead of heading across the street to my house right away, I head for Salma Harik's. When I reach the big green bin, I pat down my pockets for a pen and find a Sharpie. No paper, though. I look around for some scrap floating around. Nothing. I reach into the bin and pull out a large chunk of drywall.

Perfect. I'm writing on a piece of wall.

Dear Miss Harik,

King escaped but Noble Dog Walking found him. He is at Burlington Animal Control. Also, would you check your freezer? We think your diamond ring may have been stolen. Thank you.

Stephen Noble.

I lean the chunk of drywall against the door. She would have to move it to get inside.

At our house, Dad stands waiting with tons of new flyers. Noble Dog Walking and Cat Sitting Services.

I can't help smiling. "What changed your mind, Dad?"

"I called fifty people and no one donated."

"They all said no?"

"Thirty didn't answer. Five slammed the phone down. The others told me all the reasons why they couldn't possibly donate at this time. Some of them had such sad stories, I wanted to give *them* money."

I try to cheer him up with some good news. "We saved a couple of Mrs. Irwin's Yorkies today. Mr. Ron was walking them, and two broke free and ran across the street."

"He drove a car into the school and she gave her dogs to him? Why does she trust him over us?"

I can hear it in his voice: I've said the wrong thing, another mistake. "I don't know, but Mr. Ron thought we were heroes."

"Great, but she's the one who hires us. Listen, if this doesn't work out, don't worry. Mom told me about an air traffic control position opening up at Pearson."

No, no, no, no. I don't want Dad to go back to that. This has to work out! His mistake to mention that air traffic control job. Now I'm really going to worry.

We're the first guests at the animal shelter. I have to hand it to Ms. Lacey and her crew. They have really sparkled up the smelly beige room. Two foil cat balloons are tied to the U-shaped counter, and the floor gleams. The usual smell of animal and medicine is mixed with forest pine scent today. The cages along the walls have orange and black ribbons on them, as though the animals are Halloween presents. In a large glassed room to the right, Ms. Lacey directs someone with hand signals. Serge. We step into that room.

"Put this on. You are dealing with food!" She hands him a hairnet. "These are the cookies and squares I want on the plates. You still have to bring out the juice boxes. Instructions for the coffee are on the machine. Chop, chop!" She makes one hand into a blade that slices across her other hand quickly. Her diamond ring twinkles from the blade hand.

Serge obeys and his shaggy brown hair gets all squished down by the light-blue netting. His strange eyes and the flattened hair make him look like the housekeeper in a horror movie.

"Oh, hi there." Ms. Lacey's voice comes out way higher and friendlier as she turns to Dad. "Can I interest you in a lovely Maine coon? Totally litter trained. Loves kids."

"Sorry, my wife is allergic. But I wanted to give you these for your dogs." He holds out a bag of liver bites.

"Mmm." She sniffs at them.

"Also I want to hand out my flyers for our dog-walking and cat-sitting service. Maybe if people are nervous about owning a pet, knowing about us will help them decide."

"Yeah! Can I see one?" She looks it over and nods. "I'll put one up on our bulletin board." Her head snaps around to Serge. "Fill the coffee machine in the kitchen first. Hurry it up. We've got guests!"

He picks up the tall metal cylinder in two hands and peers around it to see. I open the door to the main office for him. He moves quickly, too quickly, just as the next person steps through the door. Mrs. Klein. She looks around, confused. She's dressed in orange and black, a strange colour combination with her red hair, but the good thing is she's also wearing dangly Halloween cat earrings. Shows her heart is in it.

Ms. Lacey brightens. "Yoo-hoo, over here!"

Mrs. Klein doesn't see the coffee machine coming at her. She swings around and smacks into Serge.

"Ow! Ow!"

There's a loud clang as the machine topples to the floor. Mrs. Klein rubs her face.

"Sorry."

The big mistake, number nine, winning over all our other ones today, belongs to Serge for moving so quickly he can't see where he's going. But at least his mistake doesn't cause any bleeding.

"Oh it's you again. I saw you on your skateboard with the paint."

DAY THREE, MISTAKE TEN

Serge doesn't answer. Instead he scrambles to pick up the coffee maker and lid. Still, deep down, I know. I take out my cell phone, key in the number of Constable Wilson, and text: *Please come to animal shelter.*

Ms. Lacey opens the door. "Are you okay? Do you need ice?"

"I'm fine," Ms. Klein answers.

"Can you be more careful!" Ms. Lacey grumps at Serge. He ignores her and continues on into the back with the coffee maker.

"Please join us for refreshments. In here." Ms. Lacey waves Mrs. Klein in our direction.

Mrs. Klein steps into the room, looking around still. "Where are the cats?"

"Oh. We have to serve the food away from the animals. Health regulations and all that." Ms. Lacey slits open a plastic tub and pops the lid. "Cookie?" she offers.

Large with white icing and a cherry on top, they look delicious.

"Don't mind if I do." Mrs. Klein takes one. "I love Empire cookies."

Ms. Lacey nods to us, and Dad and I grab a couple, too.

"We were just talking about this service." Ms. Lacey taps her hand against Dad's flyer. "Noble Cat Sitting. You might want to take one in case you find yourself a kitty."

"May I have a few?" She takes some from Ms. Lacey and glances over one. "I think Rottweiler cleaning clients might need help with their pets. I sure would prefer if the animals were being walked while I clean."

Dad smiles. Things are looking up.

"Renée's here!" I can see her and her mother walking in, Renée with a laptop bag slung over her shoulder. The surprise is that Attila and Star follow them.

Serge steps back into the front room, this time carrying what has to be a heavier coffee machine now that it's full of water.

"Watch it," I call to Renée. We learn from our mistakes. She manages to dodge Serge. His mother, our principal, Mrs. Watier, clip-clops in with her tall boots, hand in hand with Mr. Sawyer.

Renée turns to make her silent-scream face at me. Who could believe they'd become a couple again?

Mr. Sawyer flicks his fingers through his long blond bangs.

"You're just in time for the tour!" Ms. Lacey says as they come to the refreshment room. "Come on in, everyone. Have a cookie first."

Attila and Star grab some Empire cookies. Renée lifts her shoulders in a question as she points with her chin to the laptop bag.

There's no time to explain anything to her.

Serge sets the coffee machine down on the table, pushing aside a clamshell of brownies. They slide dangerously close to the edge.

"Careful!" Ms. Lacey barks at Serge as she grabs the brownie box. She grumbles as she pulls off the lid. "Have to stay on top of the kid all the time." She winks at Mrs. Watier.

Serge scowls as he crawls under the table to plug the coffee machine in. He flicks a switch and a light comes on. With his back still toward us, Serge opens another clamshell, this time of Nanaimo bars, and begins to lay them out on a paper plate.

Renée points at his head and grins.

I grin back. She seems in a way better mood. She takes a brownie.

"We have a Himalayan cat, a Maine coon, lots of tabbies, three litters of kittens, all colours. Come, follow me." Ms. Lacey sets the brownies down on the table and then leads us back to the other room.

We're in the reception area when I see Mr. Mason and Mr. Ron heading our way. Mr. Mason's tall and bald, a shiny bullet head. Mr. Ron is round and short and hides his shaggy hair with a baseball cap. Behind them is Mr. Ron's mother, also short, with a red ski jacket draped over her red flowered Muumuu.

"People are really coming! This is so exciting." Ms. Lacey clasps her hands in front of her. "Okay. Do you all want to join us?" she calls. "Coffee's not quite ready yet."

I see Red and his father heading up the walk-way, and so does Ms. Lacey. She waits for a moment. "Welcome, welcome, everyone!" She spreads open her hands as they step in. The diamond in her ring twinkles.

Red waves to Serge in the other room, but Serge ignores him.

"Just a quick tour. Then you can all visit with the animals. Have a coffee or a juice and maybe take home a pet." She leads us around the reception area first. "These are the small animals. As you can see, we have some ferrets and a mouse."

"So cute," Renée says about the white, red-eyed rodent. Its nose twitches our way. A perfect girl-friend for Mickey.

Behind the cage I see a patch of white paint — the drywall repair. Where is Harry? I wonder, look-ing toward the door.

Mrs. Irwin walks up the path just then. Dad pulls open the front door for her. She nods her thanks.

"As you know, we rescue animals. Down this hall we have a ball python that we just picked up. He's stubborn. Won't eat the food I've set out for him, so we make sure to keep him away from the small animals."

Good thing!

She leads us through the door and into the room where the dogs and cats are. "And over here, we have our cats. Every spring and summer, owners of un-spayed cats dump their unwanted kitten litters on us ..."

A huge raccoon-coloured cat with one eye hisses our way.

"Don't mind Bandit. He's a bit of a scrapper!" she tells us. "Our Maine coon."

"He shows such character," Mrs. Klein says, her face opening like a ball of sunshine.

Reuven and his dad join us. I wave to him. Ms. Lacey gazes happily at the small crowd around her.

"These are our kittens." Behind the bars, an orange puffball tumbles over a velvety black baby with white paws. A calico kitty sits mewing at us. A tiger stripe tests his jumping skills over a pile of snoozers. "If you adopt any of our cats, you have to promise to neuter them, but that's free with the Cat-astrophe coupon."

I want to adopt them all, but of course I can't ever own a pet of my own — Mom's allergies.

The door opens behind us and Mr. Rupert marches in, joining our group. Mrs. Klein doesn't notice; she's still visiting with Bandit, scratching at his ear through the bars. I can't help notice that he straightens up tall when he sees her.

"Over here is Snowball, who loves kids." She points to Bandit's cage mate. "Tripod in this cage is happy and healthy except for one missing front leg. Gets along perfectly fine without it. Tiger loves dogs; we actually let him visit them so he can play." She leads us to the dog hall, where all but two of the cages are empty. From those, a couple of German shepherds bark so loudly that she has to stop talking for a few moments. "Great watch dogs!" she shouts and leads us back.

In the front area Ping and Pong wag happily beside a sweaty-looking Mrs. Bennett. She's walked the whole way over?

"Feel free to visit with the animals. Have some refreshments ..."

Ping yips, encouraging me. "Wait!" I say. "I need to tell everyone about Noble Dog Walking ..."

Ms. Lacey nods and hands me some flyers. She thinks I'm going to talk about walking and looking after their pets. She is wrong. Mistake number ten.

TOO MANY MISTAKES TO COUNT

"Yesterday, while walking with those dogs" — I point to Ping and Pong — "I made an important discovery." As I unbutton my pocket, Harry, the drywall company owner, wanders in and I stop for a moment, unnerved. Behind him, a woman looks at me with sad, brown eyes. She forces a half-smile as she lifts her long black hair over her collar.

That brave smile encourages me. I raise the red cell phone high. "This device belongs to you." I hand it over to Mr. Mason. "Renée?" I take the laptop bag and remove the broken laptop to give to him as well. To the audience, I say, "Mr. Mason made a mistake. He drove off in his truck with his phone and laptop on the roof."

"Not true! It was in my office. Ronnie, here" — he thumbs toward Mr. Ron — "put it there. Someone …" He eyes Dad. "Took it."

"No, actually, I found your laptop in the bush," Attila calls. "I didn't know it was yours. But I wanted to save it for my next project. The shattered screen can represent so many things."

Mr. Ron's face flushes tomato soup red. "Um, sorry. I remember now. When I was vacuuming the truck, I stowed them on top, just for a minute. I was going to take them in the office, like you told me. But then you came out. You were in a hurry …"

Mr. Mason's jaws clench. He shakes his head.

"Clearly, Mr. Mason and Mr. Ron both made mistakes," I say. "But this isn't just about their mistakes. It's about a lot of mistaken conclusions people are making about Noble Dog Walking. Other things have gone missing, too. Your seven hundred dollars." I point to Mrs. Bennett. "From a cookie jar in the cupboard."

Perfect timing. In that moment, constables Jurgensen and Wilson step in.

"Just because Noble Dog Walking has your keys doesn't mean we're responsible for your missing electronics and cash. Unfortunately, the police can't dust it for prints, because I know I touched the cookie jar."

"Nobody stole your money." Harry, the drywall guys, jumps in now. "Remember how you promised you would pay me Saturday? You weren't home when I called. I needed that money, so I went to your stash."

Mrs. Bennett blushes. "I brought your money today!"

"I can't get an apartment without first and last months' payment," he answers. "I couldn't wait."

I interrupt. "That takes care of that crime. Then there's the case of the missing Mr. Universe medal."

"I don't care about that," Mr. Sawyer says. "I wouldn't have reported that crime, even. It's worthless."

"But *I* reported it to the police," Mrs. Irwin says. "And to my insurance company."

"Well, let's cancel that," Mr. Sawyer says. "I know who did it and I don't want to press charges."

"But what about your gym?" Harry asks him.

"Who cares about it?" He swings the hand that's holding Mrs. Watier's in the air. "I have everything I need right now. Everybody." He looks at her and then his eyes move over to Serge.

"Maybe you don't care that Serge took your medal," I say. "But what about the cars he sprayed?"

Mrs. Watier gasps.

"You can't prove anything," Serge says.

"I saw you skateboarding with that can of paint," Mrs. Klein calls.

"Says you!"

"Says me, too," Red says. "I saw him spray-paint a red truck."

"Which caused me to rush to have it cleaned, which made me lose my phone and laptop!" Mr. Mason says.

Serge turns and really gives Red an intense stare. "I let you hang around, you pile of …"

"You're not teaching me skateboarding like you promised," Red says.

Constable Jurgensen steps between them. "Actually, we know you did it, Serge. Mr. Rupert turned in the paint can and we found your prints, which we had on file because of the dognapping and mischief charges against you already."

"Which leaves us with one other mystery. How did a ball python get from Overton Court all the way to Duncaster Park?" I ask.

"He slithered over?" suggests Serge. "I didn't have anything to do with any snake."

Renée grabs Attila's arm. "Was it you?"

"No. I never saw any ball python in the park or anywhere else."

"Then what did you source for your graffiti in the pipe at the park?"

"The app we were testing on my cell." He points to the woman with the long black hair. "Salma Harik designed it. It inspired me."

"It is truly a beautiful snake. You all saw it over there." Ms. Lacey gestures with her hand and her diamond flashes.

Suddenly, there's a scream.

"You gave away my ring!" Salma Harik cries and pushes Harry, the drywaller, hard.

"No, no. I never gave it to her. I sold it!"

She shoves him even harder. "How could you do that so quickly? We just broke up."

"Saturday morning, ten fifteen. You said we were definitely through this time. I needed a place to live. None of my clients were paying."

I would almost feel sorry for him except for

one thing. "You were the one who dumped King in the park."

"It had to be him," Renée agrees with me. "No way could he have slithered there on his own."

"I hate that stupid snake!" Harry shouts, which is a mistake. It is like confessing.

Ms. Lacey gasps. "How could you be so cruel!"

"It was warm out. He survived."

"No thanks to you," Salma says.

Constable Jurgensen corrals Serge. I see handcuffs flash.

"Do you want to press charges?" Constable Wilson asks Salma.

She shakes her head.

"What about you, Miss?" she asks Mrs. Bennett.

"I think it's really high-handed to come into my house to collect your money. Without even asking," she tells Harry.

It was a mistake, I think. Definitely a bad one.

"Shall I arrest him?" Constable Wilson asks.

"No. I was going to pay him. I just got called for another flight and headed out quickly."

Not paying on time as promised is another mistake. I've lost count of how many errors the adults have all made.

Constable Jurgensen leads Serge out the door. Constable Wilson follows. Mrs. Watier and Mr. Sawyer leave behind them. Everyone talks among themselves and it's hard get their attention again. "Excuse me, excuse me."

Finally, Renée puts a thumb and pointer finger in her mouth and whistles louder than I've ever heard anyone whistle before. They all go quiet.

"What I want to point out to all of you is that Noble Dog Walking was in no way connected with any of the crimes. If anything, we helped solve them. So if you want to hire some great dog walkers or cat sitters, please take a flyer!"

I hold them up in the air.

Mr. Rupert, of all people, takes the first one. "I'm adopting Bandit. I've never seen such a tough-looking cat."

"He is a character!" Mrs. Klein winks. "A strong cat. We are co-owning him." She tucks her arm in Mr. Rupert's. "I'm sure I have the Noble Dog Walking number so I don't need a flyer."

Mr. Mason steps up. "Look, I'm really sorry about accusing your dad. Just that he walked Bailey and suddenly I couldn't find my phone."

Mrs. Ron marches in and whaps him with a flyer. "You should be sorry. You too, Ronnie!"

"But I didn't say he stole the laptop and phone! I forgot all about putting them on top of the truck, honest, I did," Mr. Ron says. He turns to Dad, who is surrounded by other people. "I'm sorry you were blamed," he calls to him.

Dad shrugs.

"Thanks for telling me about Cat-astrophe," Mr. Mason continues. "I'm adopting Tiger. He and Bailey can keep each other company."

"Let's get a kitty, too, Ma. Can we?" Mr. Ron asks.

"Yup, yup, yup. Good idea. Living back of the park we get too many mice this time of year."

"Stephen, speaking of mice," Renée says. "I have a surprise for you."

the
aftermath

Renée tugs at my arm.

"Just a minute. My mother's coming up the walkway!" I rush to open the door of the animal shelter. "What are you doing? You're going to get sick if you come in here."

"Hey, we vacuumed and cleaned every inch of this place," Ms. Lacey says. "By we, I mean I got that kid Serge to do it."

Mom comes into the reception area still wearing her navy-blue airline pantsuit. "I took some antihistamines. If I remember not to touch my face or rub my eyes, I should be fine."

"Hey, I have something that will help." While Mom and I hug, Ms. Lacey ducks behind the counter and pulls open a drawer. "Try these!" She brings over some goggles, and before Mom can say anything, pulls them over her head and adjusts the strap. "They have to fit snug."

Mom looks like a crazy human fly. She smiles.

Even more people drift in as I introduce Mom to Renée's mother. Dad's still surrounded by people taking our flyers.

"I know you're allergic and everything, so I hope you won't mind," Renée starts, "but my mom and I agreed we would like to adopt Minnie mouse over in the corner for Stephen. He'll stay at our house and keep Mickey company. Minnie that is, not Stephen. Although Stephen can sleep over sometimes."

"Wow. That's generous of you. What do you say, Stephen?" Mom turns to me.

"Yeah! That would be great. My own pet!"

Ms. Lacey hurries over to us. "It's going really well! A friend of yours is adopting Tripod!"

"Who?" I ask.

"Guy over there." She points to Reuven and his dad. Then she waves her hand and calls out, "Coffee's ready, everyone! Please help yourselves to more treats."

Even with the goggle solution, Mom seems happy to step into the glassed-off refreshment area. Renée and her mom join us. Star and Attila step in the room, too.

Mr. Kowalski stands beside the brownies, sipping at a coffee, looking a little sweaty from his jog over. "I can't decide whether I want the black kitten or the calico one. I wonder what colour Picasso's cat was."

"Oh, he owned several," Renée answers.

"She's right," Attila says and shrugs. "My sister's always right."

"You should adopt at least two if you want to paint like Picasso." Star winks at Mr. Kowalski.

"I like that idea, actually. Even though I don't want to paint like anyone else except myself."

Dad finally makes it into the refreshment area. "Nice glasses!" He squeezes in to give Mom a kiss. "How was your flight in?"

"Uneventful, good," she answers.

Mrs. Bennett comes over and says hi to Mom. They work together sometimes, which is how we got her as a client.

Ping and Pong jump all over Renée and me. We crouch down and I pat Pong. He can't get enough. Ping licks both of our faces and flips on his back for a belly rub.

Mrs. Bennett smiles. "I hope you two will continue walking them for me. I am so sorry about what happened. I never wanted to quit Noble Dog Walking. It's just the police suggested I have no contact until they solved the crime."

Dad chucks me on the shoulder. "Good work getting all our customers back. Noble Dog Walking has so many new clients, we may need another walker."

"If you need a snake sitter, put us down!" Attila says. "I love the way their tongues flicker."

"I'll make a note of that," Dad says. "Mrs. Irwin paid up for the dog sweaters, too."

"Yay!" Renée says, and we all toast with our Empire cookies.

People learn from their mistakes, I think. Mouth full of crumble, I grab an apple juice box and pass one to Renée.

"It was amazing how you figured out that phone and laptop thing," Dad says as he bites into a cookie. He takes a drink box from the table, too.

"Well, it helped that Ping found the phone in that corner hedge," I explain.

"Good that my brother found the laptop, too!" Renée pipes in, smiling at Attila.

"It would have made an amazing piece in his art installation," Star adds.

"I can't believe people would ever suspect Noble Dog Walking," Mom says to Dad.

"A mistake for sure," I say. "But some mistakes are lucky."

"Really?" Star says.

Ms. Lacey comes in, rubbing her hands. "We've found homes for every one of the cats. Someone's looking at the dogs, too!"

"I guess we wouldn't have handed out those Cat-astrophe flyers if Harry hadn't made his snake mistake."

"That's for sure. And I really solved the laptop and phone crime because of someone else's big boo-boo."

"What do you mean?" Mom asks.

"Well, if Mrs. Whittingham hadn't left her purse and diaper bag on the roof of the van while backing

up, I would have never connected the missing technology with the truck cleaning."

"Here's to the great mistakes we all make!" Dad
raises a juice box. Mom, Mrs. Kobai, Star, and Attila
join him, quickly grabbing juice boxes of their own.

Renée and I raise ours, too. I squeeze a little too
tightly and the juice dribbles down my hand. But
I don't care! We all touch our juice boxes together.

"To great mistakes!" Renée and I call out.

"And the mysteries we solve with them!" I cheer.

THE GREAT MISTAKE

MYSTERIES

SOME PEOPLE COUNT THEIR BLESSINGS, BUT STEPHEN NOBLE COUNTS HIS MISTAKES.

THE GREAT MISTAKE MYSTERIES

BY SYLVIA MCNICOLL

BOOK 1

BOOK 2

BOOK 3

IS IT A MISTAKE TO GIVE IN TO DOGNAPPERS?

ART IS MISSING FROM THE NEIGHBOURHOOD. HELP STEPHEN AND RENÉE CATCH THE CRIMINAL.

CAN STEPHEN AND RENÉE SOLVE THE CASE OF THE MISSING PYTHON?

THEY'RE DOGGONE GOOD MYSTERIES!